STRESS FAMILY ROBINSON

Adrian Plass

STRESS FAMILY ROBINSON

Marshall Pickering
An Imprint of HarperCollins*Publishers*

Marshall Pickering is an Imprint of
HarperCollins*Religious*
Part of HarperCollins*Publishers*
77–85 Fulham Palace Road, London W6 8JB

First published in Great Britain
in 1995 by Marshall Pickering

1 3 5 7 9 10 8 6 4 2

Copyright © 1995 Adrian Plass

Adrian Plass asserts the moral right to be
identified as the author of this work

A catalogue record for this book is
available from the British Library

ISBN 0 551 02944 7

Typeset at The Spartan Press Ltd,
Lymington, Hants
Printed and Bound in Great Britain by
HarperCollinsManufacturing Glasgow

This book is dedicated to my son, David, who first used the phrase 'Stress Family Robinson' in 1993 when all six Plasses were touring Queensland, Australia. Long hot periods of travelling in the close confines of a relatively small vehicle may well have contributed to David's small but productive burst of creativity.

Chapter One

Let me introduce you to the Robinson family. They go to the same church as I do, which is where I first met them. There are five of them, or seven if you include the two stick-insects, which Felicity Robinson always does. You'll hear quite a lot about those stick-insects later. By the way, I'm not a Robinson myself, although I think, if you asked them, all the family would say that I am nearly one – you'll hear a fair bit about that before we've finished, too. In fact, if you were talking to Felicity, she'd probably say I was absolutely, definitely another Robinson, so, just to confuse you, there are either five, six, seven or eight Robinsons, depending on who you include and who you're talking to.

I'll give myself the benefit of the doubt and start with me, because I'm the one who's telling this story.

My name is Elizabeth Reynolds, although nobody has called me Elizabeth since I was a very small girl, when I was nicknamed 'Dip' by my family for reasons which – yes, you guessed it – you'll hear about later. I'm fifty years old, but not inside, and I was born and grew up in the city of Adelaide in Australia. Nowadays I live in a little terraced house on my own in Standham, the same market town as the Robinsons, in the south of England. I was trained as a nurse, and I think I'm quite a good one, but I've only worked part time at the local hospital for a few years now, and I shall carry on doing that for as long as I can afford it. I enjoy work, but I enjoy lots of other things as well. None of my own family are alive any more, and the people I love most in the world are God and the Robinsons (I hope it's in that order). I drive a yellow mini called 'Daffodil' because I always wanted one, and the things I enjoy doing most are reading, walking, dreaming and being with the people I love most. Although I laugh a lot when I'm with my friends, I do get very lonely and unhappy sometimes, but I've become a bit of an expert at covering it up – that's one of my main faults. I've never been married so I've never had any children. I wish I had.

When I look in a mirror (I try not to) I see a tallish, rather overweight person who used to have quite a nice figure, but gets bored with living on cottage cheese and crispbread and horrible pink flavoured stuff. There's a reasonably nice, smiley, quite wide face stuck on top of the body, with light blue eyes, a full mouth and fair hair cut short because I get so sick of trying to do something with it. I do like my nose. My nose has style.

One more thing – I love being cuddled, but only by people I like, and it doesn't happen often because I don't look as if I need to be.

The man in the Robinson clan is called Mike. He's in his mid-forties, a fairly tall, nicely shaped sort of chap with a pleasant, mild expression (he goes a sort of plum colour on the rare occasions when he's angry) and reddish-gold hair that's beginning to get a bit see-through on top. For the last two years Mike has been deputy headmaster at a little village junior school two or three miles to the west of Standham. I've never actually been to Mike's school, but from the way he talks about it I should think it's a very calm and well-organized place indeed. I'm sure that all the people there, staff members and children, know exactly where they should be and what they should be doing at any given moment during the day. Mike's wife, Kathy, tells me that her husband's school is a place where naughtiness hardly happens at all. She says that Mike's disciplinary methods consist of either a stern look, which, in this setting, reduces the offending junior to a quivering wreck, or a very slightly raised voice, which presumably leaves him or her for dead. One of the great frustrations of Mike's life is that the regime and atmosphere of his place of work is impossible to duplicate in his own home. Every now and then he declares war on the formless entity which is the Robinson household, producing lists and complex plans designed to transform daily living into something efficient, smooth-running and civilized. He enrages Kathy once every month or so by suggesting that major organizational problems (he means housework) would be solved if she were to introduce some kind of system into her work. These occasional, frenetic attempts to take a dustpan and brush to the untidiness of life are largely ignored by the rest of the family, who know quite well that Mike's lists and plans will be in the bin within forty-eight hours as long as he's not encouraged.

Mike's Christianity is a little bit similar really. He

would love the whole thing to be neat and easily manageable, but he does accept – he *has* to accept, as Kathy's husband and the father of three very different children – that life is simply not like that. I don't want to give the wrong idea. Mike is a real Jesus man. He wants to do things right, and he wants to be good, it's just that the pedantic side of him takes over at times. Above all else he is an immensely kind person, who adores his family and genuinely cares about others. I love him for the gentleness and warmth he has shown me.

Definitely one of those people I like to be hugged by.

Kathy Robinson used to be a journalist before her youngest child was born six years ago. Apart from the fact that they both love travelling (and are lucky enough to be able to afford to do quite a lot of it because of money inherited from Kathy's mum and dad) she is different from her husband in just about every way that I can think of. I don't mean that the bond between them is not strong. It is strong, but it jolly well needs to be, to chain such opposites together. He's fair and she's dark; he's generally quite placid in temperament, while she swings wildly from optimism or flippancy to misery and despair; he likes things to be well organized and properly planned, she acts by instinct or inspiration, which, of course, tends to result in great successes and spectacular failures; Mike is essentially an uncomplicated person, whereas Kathy's personality is full of twists and turns and troubles, probably because of the difference in their backgrounds. Kathy's peace, as you will discover, is continually being ambushed by her own childhood trauma, in contrast to Mike, who tells people that he grew up in an atmosphere of 'quiet approval'. Kathy reckons that the approval was not as quiet as all that. She told me the story once of how, at an early stage in their courtship, she visited Mike's parents' home at Christmas time. Mike volunteered to blow up some balloons, and was half-way through inflating the first one, when his mother, who had been watching her son with fond admiration, whispered, 'My goodness, the *breath* in the boy!'

My friend is often very funny, very beautiful when things are going all right, and a staunch ally when troubles come, but she's also a stormy child who is stuck with being a grown-up. She loves her family and is often infuriated beyond measure by them, in particular by Mark, who was so solidly at the centre of his own universe at the time I'm writing about, that he repeatedly brought out all the worst feelings of inadequacy that have plagued Kathy since she first had children.

Kathy must have exhausted God over the years, but I'm sure he's crackers about her.

Finally, she just *loves* Bristol Cream sherry – and so do I.

Jack – yes, his name really is *Jack* Robinson! – is Mike and Kathy's oldest son, and I have always found him utterly delightful. Nineteen years old, you're meeting him at a time when he's moving towards the end of a year out between school and university, during which he's done just enough paid work to avoid excessive hassle from his parents. Tall, long haired and lean, very much like his father in general looks, Jack's easy contentment (and waste of milk – read on!) madden Kathy occasionally, but he's warm and affectionate as well, so she never stays mad with him for long. Jack is at that stage in his life when wisdom and naïvety are constantly elbowing each other aside. Terrific insights and intelligence are coupled with plain silliness, especially when it comes to Mark, with whom he is in a state of virtually unrelieved conflict. Jack's love of somewhat obscure music is probably the most important thing in his life, but his little sister Felicity comes a very close second, and I'm sure the music would be instantly stilled if, for some bizarre reason, a choice needed to be made. That's all I'm going to say about Jack for now.

Mark Robinson is fourteen. Writers of textbooks on parenting who want to specify this age as one that's likely to be difficult could photograph Mark in sullen mood and use him to illustrate their point. He is dark, not very tall for his age, quite broad, and as much like his mother as Jack is like his dad. He is actually a very nice looking boy, but an aura of glowering tension, mainly in the company of adults, tends to obscure this fact a lot of the time. His best friend could not deny that Mark is sometimes quite breathtakingly rude and obtuse. I think this is largely because, like many people of his age, he vaguely believes that the rest of the world (when he notices them) are there merely to swell crowd scenes in which M. Robinson is the central star. Kathy finds him very difficult indeed, and that's putting it mildly.

Most of Mark's free time is spent with his friends, a shadowy group of contemporaries, who seem to drift around our town in the late evenings from one shopwindow-lit whispering point to another in a sort of solid block of conspiring boyhood. I don't suppose they ever do anything very wicked, but they look as if they might. Mark enjoys watching some sports but he isn't very interested in taking part, so most of his energies and interests (apart from kite-flying) are bound up with these friends of his, although he too adores Felicity. He has a good but strangely quiet relationship with his dad.

I'm quite convinced that, as he gets older, Mark will be able to reveal a lot more of the sensitivity that is already there beneath the glowering and crossness. He and I have a good friendship – as long as I keep to the 'rules' – and I hope I still know him when he's older. He's going to be a terrific fellow.

Finally (if we don't include the stick-insects, and I'm not going to in this bit), there's Felicity. Felicity Robinson is six years old, fair haired, shiny-eyed, full of energy and has undoubtedly benefited from the healthy neglect that her older brothers lacked. One of the happiest people I've ever met, she brings in her turn great happiness to those she lives with, and to me. Somehow, the best of Mike and Kathy seems to have been poured into this little girl, and if you think I'm going over the top – well, I don't care. She's a little bit naughty sometimes, and I expect there'll be problems as the years go by, but in the meantime –

Felicity is wonderful. In knowing this smallest Robinson I've come closer than I ever thought possible to having a child of my own, and I thank God for her.

There you are, then – those are the Robinsons, and the following pages are all about them and the turbulent way in which they conduct their lives. There's quite a bit about me as well, because I am, after all, entitled to put D.H.R. after my name. What does D.H.R. stand for? I'm not going to tell you – read on and you'll find out.

Chapter Two

There are lots of things about being married that I really like the idea of, but I think some things would drive me completely round the bend. Take, for instance, the way in which husbands and wives seem to have the same arguments over and over again without ever realizing that their word battles have more or less become scripted. The Robinsons are extraordinary in this respect. I never stop marvelling at the way they begin each disagreement as though it's a totally new experience. It's rather sweet I suppose, but an awful waste of time usually.

A good example is the Great Packing Debate. In all the time that I've known them, this regularly repeated row has never varied by more than a word or two, and it always ends in exactly the same way. I love them both dearly, but, in battle mode, Mark and Kathy can be startlingly predictable.

I first witnessed this particular piece of unconsciously rehearsed role-play on a Saturday when the family were due to disappear for a long holiday over the Easter period. Knowing that the packing for America had been put off again and again, and, incredibly, would somehow have to be fitted in before lunch, I'd offered to pop round after breakfast to see if I could help. Arriving at the Robinsons' tall thin Victorian semi-detached at about nine o'clock, I found six-year-old Felicity glowing prettily in the spring sunshine on top of a brick pillar by the gate as she addressed an invisible circle of admirers.

'You are all my very good friends,' she was saying graciously, as I stepped out of Daffodil and locked the door behind me, 'and I love every one of you exactly the same amount. You are all invited to my next birthday party, which will be horse-riding, swimming, jungle-tumble, bowling, ice-skating and deep-pan pizzas.'

'Can I come?' I asked.

'No, Dip,' said Felicity, 'you can come to my real party, which will be Daddy doing tricks that don't work and Mummy getting cross because people won't play the games properly – and a nice tea', she added, anxious to be absolutely fair.

'Mummy and Daddy up yet?'

'Drinking coffee in the kitchen and sighing and making lists. Jack's gone back upstairs with his headphones on because Mummy said his room looked as if something sad and terrible had happened there.'

'Oh, dear! And Mark?'

'Mark got very cross because he said no one had told him we were going to America today and he'd arranged to go out with his friends. Mummy said only a deaf imbecile could've not known we were going, and if Mark was's interested in his family as he is in his blinking friends he might have a better idea of what was going on. Then Mark said that next time boring guests came round he wouldn't bother to be polite, and he stomped off with his feet sticking out, like a duck in a sulk, and Mummy said she

would never have believed that the back of someone's head could be so infuriating.' – Felicity sighed
– 'It hasn't been a very good morning, really.'

'It doesn't sound very good,' I agreed, 'but I'm
sure it'll get better. It's always difficult when you go
away. I've come to lend a hand.'

'You'll have to wait till they've had their packing
argument,' said Felicity, solemnly, 'nothing'll
happen till they've had that. We've got a secret
surprise for you later', she added mysteriously.

'Oooh, well, I shall look forward to that, I like
surprises!'

I found Mike and Kathy slumped over coffee
mugs and pieces of paper at the kitchen table. They
looked haggard and depressed, not at all like people
who were planning to fly to America for a family
holiday in a few hours' time. The kitchen looked as
if it had drunk too much the night before and woken
up wishing it hadn't.

'Hello, Dip,' said Mike, getting up, 'I'm afraid
we're not in a very good state this morning –
haven't really got moving. You sit down and I'll
make you a coffee. One sugar at the moment, isn't
it? We're just writing a list of things to do and
then – '

'And then,' interrupted Kathy, clutching fistfuls
of dark hair close to her scalp, 'we pack three weeks'
worth of luggage that should have been done a week
ago, scrape the grease off this infernal pit – '

'We prayed over this kitchen when we moved in,
Kath,' interposed Mike mildly, setting a coffee of
typically Robinsonian darkness before me, 'I don't

think you ought to call it an infernal pit. What do you think, Dip?'

'I don't think it – '

'Then,' continued Kathy, 'we'll have a long theological discussion about how to avoid hurting the saintly kitchen's feelings, followed by some sort of attempt to mend our fractured domestic situation. Next we'll clean the house up – that should only take about four hours, then we'll do the things we shall have undoubtedly forgotten about, and then, assuming that our dear sons will be generous enough to accompany us, we'll set off, intending to go to the airport, but knowing in our hearts that, in fact, we are heading for a pre-ordained spot in the middle of nowhere, miles from a garage, where our sad vehicle will lie down and die. And that,' concluded Kathy, releasing her hair and bringing her fists down on the table with a thump, 'apart from my intention to inflict serious injury on the deaf imbecilic duck if and when it returns, completes the itinerary for today.'

'Kath finds going away a bit difficult', said Mike, rather unnecessarily. 'You haven't started your coffee yet, Dip. Is it okay?'

I shrugged noncommittally. 'It's err . . . it's still a tiny bit strong for me, Mike. Nice, but strong. Look won't you let me help you?' I laid a hand on Kathy's arm. 'I would really and truly love to stay behind after you've gone, and sort the kitchen and the rest of the house out. I like being in other people's houses – I honestly do.'

Kathy gave a weary little whimper as hope battled with politeness. 'Oh, Dip, you don't want . . . .'

'Apart from anything else,' I went on persuasively, 'it'll give me a chance to look through all your private papers and poke my nose into things that don't concern me. Please don't deprive me of that opportunity. People in the church would love to hear a few iffy things about you – just in confidence and for prayer, of course.'

Kathy's changes of mood always reminded me of the weather in Melbourne, where I lived when I was training. Suddenly the sun came out as she threw her head back and laughed. 'You're on! Make sure you put Mike's pornography back where you find it, though, won't you?'

'Kath!' Mike was very nearly annoyed. 'I *never* look at that sort of magazine at all – I wouldn't dream of having anything like that in my house. I can't remember ever looking at – well, I suppose if I'm absolutely honest, when I was young . . . ' Mike's fresh complexion turned a deep, rich, red colour, 'I might have glanced occasionally at – well . . . some picture that a friend had, or something, but certainly not err . . . now. Certainly not.'

'You don't have to do your giant radish impression, Mike. Dip knows I was only joking, don't you, Dip?'

'Well, yes,' I replied, 'but I was just thinking that I've got plenty of pornography of my own.'

They stared at me in surprise. 'You have?' said Mike.

'Certainly – up here.' I tapped my head. 'Lots of it up there. You don't flick all the switches to "off" just because you've gone past fifty, you know. It's a bit of a nuisance sometimes. Anyway, never mind me – the point is, you're going to let me stay behind and clean up for you, aren't you? That'll leave you free to sort the packing out and do anything else that needs doing.'

Mike was obviously still wrestling with the idea that single middle-aged ladies might sometimes battle with pornographic fantasies, but his face was almost its normal colour again. 'Well, if you're sure, Dip . . .'

'I'm sure.'

'She's sure', said Kathy, standing up decisively. 'Let's get on with the packing.'

Mike got to his feet as well, but as they faced each other across the table I sensed that a new tension had introduced itself. Could it be that the essential Packing Argument mentioned by Felicity was about to get under way?

It was. Mike launched it.

'Darling, let's be really systematic this time. We've got five large suitcases altogether, haven't we?'

Kathy's jaw moved soundlessly for a moment. Her fingers drummed quietly on the edge of the table. 'What was wrong with the way we did it last time?'

Mike moved away towards the window, one hand raised in silent pre-emphasis as he mustered his arguments. I don't know if you've met people like Mike. If you have, you'll know that, whilst generally mild and non-confrontational, they can become quite feverishly obsessional about the most trivial things. Even now, at this early stage in the forthcoming debate, Mike was quivering with restrained passion. Strange, but true.

'Well, come on,' repeated Kathy irritably, 'tell me what was wrong with the way we did it when we went to France.'

Mike turned to face his wife, gripping the front edge of the window sill behind him with both hands, as if frightened that, inflated by his passion, he might ascend slowly to the ceiling and hang there like a helium balloon.

'Nothing much – it's just that I can't get involved when you organize it. We end up in a sea of clothes and shoes and books and bits and pieces, with the cases buried somewhere underneath, and I wade dismally through it all with a teacloth in my hand wondering where it fits into your master plan.'

Mike was really motoring now, bobbing up and down on his heels very rapidly, and sounding like a man who has been brought face to face with some dreaded, ultimate emotional crisis.

'I don't know where anything is!' he continued wildly, 'I don't know where anything goes – I don't know what's going on, and I – '

Kathy finished her husband's sentence acidly. 'And you start shaking your head and hissing through your teeth and talking about how your wonderfully organized childhood makes it very difficult for you to cope with chaos.'

In the short silence that followed, Kathy slumped back into her seat, put her elbows on the table, and rested her chin wearily in her hands.

'I *don't* do that', said Mike, his eyes wide with outrage.

Kathy didn't even look at him. 'You're almost doing it now, and we haven't even started yet.'

Mike turned stiffly and stared out of the window, exercising what must have seemed to him heroic self-control. 'Look, all I'm saying is that we could try it my way and see how we get on – just try it, for goodness' sake. That's all I'm saying.'

'Your way being what, exactly?'

Pleased with the opportunity to explain, Mike swung round and began to pace the length of the kitchen, addressing Kathy as though she was an infant class.

'We take all five cases out into the garden, right? And – '

'And we put them in a nice neat row – ' Kathy seemed to know what was coming.

'We put them in a row with the lids open, and we number them from one to five, and agree about what sort of luggage is going into each one, then we bring stuff out from the house bit by bit and fill the cases until there's nothing left in the house that should be in the cases. Apart from anything else it would be so much more fun doing it this way. You'd say to me, "Here's a shirt, Mike, it goes in number three", and I go out and put it in number three. Then you might say, "Here's a pair of shoes, Mike, they go in number five", so I put them in number five and come back for the next thing, and so on. Then we could swop round and I'd say, "Here's a blouse, Kath, it goes in number four", and you'd go out and put it in number four, then you'd come back for the next thing, and so on.'

Kathy groaned, as if she was in pain.

'Then, when everything's in, we shut the cases and that's that. The packing's done, everything's ready and we haven't had to hack our way through forests of overcoats and underwear just to find the floor.'

Emboldened by what he obviously felt to be the overwhelming force of his own logical argument, Mike ceased his pacing, sat down opposite Kathy again and invited her to submit to reason.

'How can you say that doesn't make sense, Kath? How can it possibly *not* make sense? How? Well, how can it? Come on – tell me how it can possibly not make sense. It seems so obvious. Surely you can see that, can't you?'

Folding her arms and leaning back in her chair, Kathy looked into her husband's imploring eyes and spoke with implacable calm.

'Michael, I wish to make the following observations. First of all, let us consider the difference between your method and mine. Your system may be neat and logical, but it would take about a year to get everything packed. In fact, it would become more of an ongoing hobby than a functional task. My method, on the other hand, may appear wild and unfathomable and cause you unspeakable anguish, but it would mean the packing gets done *before* we leave for America – an attractive little feature of my approach, wouldn't you say? Furthermore, touched though I am by the picture of you and me trotting happily and eternally to and fro with shirts and blouses and pairs of shoes, I have no intention of playing "Jane And John Go On Their Holidays" out in the garden just to pander to your completion neurosis. You may not know what's going on when I pack, but I do. And as it's always me that ends up doing it anyway, that's all that really matters, isn't it? Why don't you give Dip a hand with the kitchen and leave me to do the packing, then you won't have to worry about it at all, will you? How does that sound?'

'So you don't want me to help?'

Something told me that we had reached the real point of the discussion at last.

'Of course I'd like you to help – if you really mean it. What I can't stand is having you huffing and puffing around getting upset about not being able to do anything while I'm busy *doing* it.'

'Oh, well . . . ,' said Mike, sounding hurt, but not very convincingly so, 'I might just as well stay here and help Dip, then, if that's how you feel about it. By the way, Dip, what do *you* think of my way of doing it?'

I wanted to make real friends with the Robinsons.

'Ridiculous,' I smiled, 'charming, but ridiculous. Leave it to Kathy.'

I loved the way they both laughed.

Later, as Mike and I tackled the sink section of the 'infernal pit' side by side, I talked to him about the Packing Argument.

'It was almost', I said, 'as though you had to go through all that just so that you'd arrive at a place where you knew you'd end up anyway. I don't think there was ever any question of you helping with the packing – not, I hasten to add, that you didn't mean what you said, of course, Mike. You've obviously got very strong views on how to fill suitcases. I'm very unformed in that area. I have none at all.'

Mike chuckled. He was back to his cheery, unruffled self again.

'We are a bit silly sometimes, I suppose. Kath worries that we haven't got one of those perfect Christian marriages that you read about in books, but, well . . . we do love each other. That's pretty important, isn't it?' He suddenly gave a little embarrassed cough, and put down the plate he was polishing. 'It must be very hard for you sometimes, Dip – I mean, you must get sick of people going on about their wives and husbands and all that, when you . . . '

'When I've never married? Yes, it is a bit difficult sometimes, but I love being with families, and I don't find single living quite so bad nowadays, actually. Not being married isn't an illness, you know. To be honest, Mike, I don't know if I could stand sharing – you know – intimate space with someone else after all these years.'

Through the window I could see Felicity spinning round and round very fast on the yellow plastic swing that hung from one of the apple trees. Little girl dreams came back suddenly.

'I tell you what, though, there are times when I long for there to be someone waiting for me when I get home – someone to ask how things have gone at work, make me a cup of tea – that sort of thing. And sometimes, when I'm out at a place where there are lots of people, I wish . . . you're going to think this sounds extremely silly.'

'No,' said Mike, 'go on, I'm interested.'

I glanced quickly at his face and carried on.

'Well, I wish there was an eye to catch across the room, above the heads of the others – just for a moment – one of those small smiles that tells you someone understands exactly what you're thinking, and then you go back to chatting or whatever it is you're doing, but you know you're not on your own. Being special to someone, number one in their lives – I know it's silly, but I still cry for that every now and then.'

For a few moments the dribble of tap-water into the sink and the clink of dishes was the only sound to be heard in the Robinson kitchen, but it was not an awkward pause.

'There's one thing,' said Mike at last, 'at least you don't have to go through convoluted arguments before anything gets done, like we just did.'

'Well, no, but . . . ' I paused, suddenly a little afraid. This was very solid coin I was passing across the counter of our still developing friendship. Not the sort you can ever take back again. 'No, but we single people play our own silly little games, you know. At least – I do.'

'Such as?'

I peeled the rubber gloves from my hands and dropped them into the sink.

'Dry tea-towel?'

'In the drawer under where the stick-insects are. Acres of tea-towels. We're good at having dry tea-towels. Carry on about your little games.'

'Sometimes,' I said, reaching for a handful of wet

cutlery, 'I lose confidence in people.' I checked myself. 'Actually, that's not fair. I guess what I really mean is that I lose confidence in myself. Maybe it's a family – like yours – and I've been visiting a lot and everything seems fine, then all of a sudden I get this cold feeling in my stomach, and I think – what if they've just been putting up with me? What if they're being *kind* to me? Then I panic. And that's when the games start.'

Outside, Felicity had abandoned her swing, and was squatting down by the small flower bed that was specially her own, poking the earth with a stick. Happening to look up at that moment, she caught my eye and grinned. Why did Felicity's smile produce these spasms of choking tearfulness in me sometimes?

'I dive back into my little house like a frightened rabbit, and I shut the door behind me – lock it, bolt it, put a chair against it – anything to shut the world out so they can't see my embarrassment about being an interfering old bore who shoves herself in where she's not wanted. Then I might walk round the house with my fists clenched for a bit – have a little swear at myself, that sort of thing.'

Poor Mike had to say something, of course. 'But, Dip, you don't really think – '

'I'm not talking about what I think, Mike. I'm talking about what I *feel*. On those days I *feel* like a shapeless piece of rubbish, and I know that no one really likes me. They're just pretending, and I never want to see any of them ever again.'

'So the game is . . . ?'

'The game is – oh, I do feel a twit, Mike! The game – one of the games – is that I don't make contact with anyone for days and days, or even weeks, just to see how long it will be before they get round to remembering that I exist and write or phone or something. I know it's childish and silly, but – I suppose I just reach the bottom of myself every now and then and turn into a blob.'

'You've dried that last knife five times, Dip. Does it work?'

'Does what work? The not-making-contact, you mean? No, not really. I cuddle a load of burning resentment to myself for a bit, then I start missing people, so I go and see them and they're usually so pleased to see me, and I'm so pleased to see them that I forget all about being deeply hurt and everything gets back to normal.' I laughed. 'It backfired badly once. There was this couple in my last church but one who reckoned they had a "Ministry To Single Folk", and got very stroppy when I didn't go round for a while. They turned up at the door one evening with their mouths looking like bits of frayed string, and told me that because I had not been attending their gatherings – oh, Mike, I'd have had more fun being buried alive – they felt led to draw apart from me for a season, whatever that is. Then off they went, leaving me feeling very relieved and a bit guilty – only a bit, though.'

Mike threw the bottle-opener into its place, and closed the cutlery drawer with a triumphant bang.

'That's the washing-up done. Now we'll tackle the floor. Let's be syst–, I mean, you sweep, Dip, and I'll put the chairs up because I know how to arrange them, then you can talk to me from the hall while I mop. Okay?'

Leaning against the doorway with my arms folded a few minutes later, I felt a touch uneasy watching Mike as he worked slowly and methodically back towards me with the mop. A question was taking shape in the concentrated rhythm of his movements. If I hadn't known that the forthcoming holiday was about to create a natural gap, I might have done my rabbit act there and then. What price was I to pay for my vulnerability?

'Can I ask you something, Dip?'

'No.'

'Can I?'

I sighed. 'Yes.'

'Well – why did you tell me all that? I mean, you've blown the whatsit, haven't you? How can you go off and play games about not contacting us when we'll know exactly what you're doing, and turn up at your door with huge bunches of flowers and declarations of everlasting friendship as soon as we don't see you for more than a day or two? D'you see what I mean?'

I was determined not to cry. I took a deep breath.

'The thing is, Mike, I don't want to play games with you and Kathy and the others. I'm nearly fifty-one years old, and I don't think there's much chance of me hitching up with someone special now – not if I'm realistic. I meant it just now when I said that I couldn't imagine being that close to anyone in that way nowadays. But recently I've begun . . . '

Sensing my need to know he was with me, Mike turned round, leaned on his mop, and nodded. 'Go on, I'm listening.'

'Recently I've begun to feel lonely in a way that's different – there's a sort of panic in it, a fear that I'm going to become old without giving away – ' I struggled for a moment ' – without giving away *me* to anyone, me without the games and the unnecessary holding back and the staying calm and dependable and all that. I don't want to be a block of concrete round anyone's neck, but I would like to belong somewhere.' I stared hard at the tumble-dryer. 'You and Kathy and the kids have – how can I describe it? – you've let me be part of what's going on without tidying up your Christian act before I see it. You've let me in to where you really are, and, well, I've never really known what that feels like before. I want it to go on happening. I want that very much. Have I embarrassed you?'

Mike shifted his weight on the mop handle. 'Last night, after everyone had gone,' he said slowly and seriously, 'Kath and I were in bed, having a rather familiar end-of-the-day conversation. This particular one never changes much. She despairs about her terrible mothering and her looks and the decay of her writing talent and her ingratitude to God for what he's given her in all those areas, and I say things like, "Come on now, Kath, you know things aren't really that bad." Then she tells me what's wrong with *me*, and I listen but don't say anything – used to, but not any more – until she's said whatever's on her mind, then she usually cries, and we have a cuddle and everything's more or less all right. Well, we went through all that, and then, just as we were settling down to go to sleep, Kath suddenly said, "Mike, I wish Dip would come and live with us and be part of it all. I feel safe and warm when she's here." Those were the words she used – "safe and warm."'

He paused, searching for a way to convey the sincerity of what he was saying.

'Dip, we're a chaotic family – I don't have to tell you that. We seem to spend an awful lot of time pretending that we're more organized or more holy or more together than we really are. A waste of time, I'm sure, but I'm afraid it's the way we're made. You're the first person we haven't minded seeing us just as we are.' He smiled. 'Whether you like it or not, Miss Reynolds, you've got this warmth and acceptance about you that Kath and I just – well – just love. We both said exactly the same thing the other day. When you come in to the house everything lights up a bit.'

He turned abruptly and attacked the floor with even more vigour than before.

'This is a big old house, Dip,' he said over his shoulder, 'plenty of room for a bedsitter on the top floor. Think about it while we're in America, will you?'

'But Kathy – '

'Just now, you said that you wanted to be number one in someone's life, right? Well, I can't guarantee that, but I *can* tell you that you come an easy sixth as far as Kath's concerned – in fact, the way things are going with Mark at the moment, I should think you've been promoted to fifth. Think about it while we're away, will you? Promise?'

'I promise.'

The kitchen clock was showing exactly twenty-five minutes past two when Kathy, Mike, Jack, Felicity and I sat down at the table to a late lunch of fish and chips fetched from the High Street by Jack, whose room now looked (according to his mother) as though something sad and terrible had been poorly concealed. There was still no sign of Mark. Kathy's method must have worked pretty well because the packing was all done, but she looked very tired and grumpy.

'We won't bother having plates or anything,' said Mike slightly tensely, as he unwrapped the food, 'there's no point in cleaning everything up and then using it again. We might as well use our fingers and eat off the wrapping paper, then we can just screw the paper up and wash our hands, can't we?'

'I don't know why we *ever* bother to use plates,' commented Jack, 'it's just another way of complicating life, isn't it? As far as I'm concerned food's just a fuel. You put it in and it makes the engine work.'

He placed a large piece of fried fuel into his mouth and chewed it with visible relish.

'I like eating with my fingers,' said Felicity serenely. 'Why don't we say grace when it's just us? We never say grace unless someone's here – a *visitor*.' She pronounced the last word as though it was a dangerous disease.

'Dip is here, Felicity,' said Mike, 'doesn't she count?'

'No, silly,' replied Felicity scornfully, 'Dip *is* us. Mummy, why don't we say grace when it's just us? Do you think God only wants us to thank him for our food when someone important comes to dinner? At Emily's house they say grace before breakfast and tea and *everything*, even if there's only Emily and her mummy and me there. At Emily's house they – '

'Felicity, shut *up* about Emily's house,' interrupted Kathy irritably, 'I couldn't care less what they do at Emily's house. They're obviously much more wonderful at Emily's house than they are at Felicity's house, but I'm afraid you're stuck with living here with your own useless mother, so eat your fish and be quiet!'

In the silence that followed two huge tears welled up in Felicity's eyes and trickled slowly down her face. Mike had stopped eating and was staring at Kathy, perhaps waiting for her to repair the damage she'd done before someone else had to. Jack broke the silence. He wasn't going to stop the fuel transportation process for anything, but he had time between two mouthfuls to express a view.

'That's a bit unfair, Mum. Flitty was only pointing out how hypocritical it is to put on a show for some people and not bother with others.'

A huge forkful of fish and chips postponed Jack's developing defence of his little sister, but he wouldn't have been allowed to continue anyway. Whatever was heating up in Kathy came to the boil at that moment. Leaning across the table, she raised a rigid forefinger and jabbed it in the direction of her oldest son.

'Don't you *ever* lecture me on the subject of hypocrisy. I am an expert in that area after living with you for the last year or so. You sit there stuffing your face with chips and telling me that plates complicate life – well, let me add to your vast store of information by telling you that milk bottles complicate life as well, especially when I find five of them in that pit you call a bedroom, each with at least a quarter of a pint of rancid milk stinking the place out. When you've started clearing up your own messes and stopped wasting our money, I might be willing to listen to your views on the way we conduct our spiritual lives and bring up the rest of our children.'

There was a miserable pause. Jack put his non-fuel-injecting arm round Felicity, who was still sniffing, and Mike opened his mouth to say something. The blast was turned in his direction.

'If you're about to tell me that I've dropped a bit of fish or something on your nice, clean, blasted kitchen, Mike, I think I shall walk out of this house – I really think I will. I seem to be surrounded by neurotics and idiots who haven't got the wit to sort anything out for themselves, and I've had enough!'

Kathy placed her hands flat against her face and started to sob noiselessly, the top half of her body shaking with emotion. Felicity, red-eyed, looked at her mother in puzzlement.

'Daddy,' she said in a small, bruised voice, 'why's Mummy crying? Is she cross or upset?'

Mike spread his hands, bewildered and unhappy. 'I'm not sure, darling. Don't worry, though.

Mummy didn't mean to get so – she didn't mean what she said. She's just got a bit upset.'

'It was only four milk bottles,' offered Jack tentatively and perhaps rather empty-headedly, as though he felt it might make all the difference to the situation.

I felt terribly sorry for them all, but at the same time, inside my own head, the memory of something Felicity had said was singing like a bird – the same song over and over again: 'Dip *is* us, Dip *is* us, Dip *is* us . . . ' I was certainly the happiest person in the Robinson kitchen at that moment. I longed to help.

Something about the way Kathy was behaving brought to mind all those occasions in the past, mostly in the evenings, when a wave of panic-stricken loneliness had come crashing in to engulf whatever peace I'd achieved, leaving me gasping for air and crying for the same reason that a baby does, out of pure need. You never shared that. What you did was – you waited until the tears had stopped, then you went upstairs and washed your face and brushed your hair, and when you looked reasonably all right you went down again, sat by the phone, and thought through a list of the people you knew. When you finally got round to calling somebody you sounded bright and casual. You said you'd thought of popping round a bit later (because you'd be passing anyway) to sort something out, or make some arrangement, or pick up something you'd left there. It wasn't urgent, you'd insist. It could wait – just a thought . . .

Then, if they said it was a good idea, you listened hard to discover if they really wanted you. If they did – or if they acted it convincingly enough – you went round. When you got there they'd ask you how you were, and you'd tell them you were fine and do a little light laugh, but inside you'd be screaming silently for them to put their arms round you and love you and look after you.

I'm quite sure other people cope much better with living on their own than I used to. But experiences like mine make you very sensitive to the proposition that people might *mean* something they're not saying. I knew that Kathy's problem was nothing to do with anybody sitting in the kitchen. I leaned across and gently took one hand away from her face.

'It's Mark, isn't it?'

At that moment we all heard the sound of someone opening the front door. The absence of any corresponding sound of the front door shutting suggested that Mark had returned at last. Two seconds later he walked into the kitchen and stared at the food on the table.

'Couldn't wait for me, then?' he said indignantly.

Chapter Three

'Plenty here for you, Mark, sit down and I'll sort yours out for you.'

Mike's brave attempt to carry on as if nothing was really wrong failed almost immediately. Kathy had stopped crying. Now she was white and still with anger. Pushing her seat back she stood up and moved round until she was directly behind the chair into which Mark had casually dropped. He had already started to chomp noisily. Kathy's voice was tight with fury.

'Your father may think there's no problem, young man, but I happen to think there is.' She paused. 'Are you listening to me?'

Mark went on eating as though his mother didn't exist.

'I *said* – are you listening to me?' Another pause. 'If you don't say something to me I'm going to drag you out of that chair and *make* you answer.'

'I can hear your voice, if that's what you mean.'

The ghostly premonition of a clout round the back of the head had forced a response from the boy, but his words were just about as graceless and provocative as he could make them.

'Well, if you can hear my voice, you can hear me saying this, then, can't you? In my opinion – not that you give a monkey's about my opinion, I'm well aware of that – your behaviour has made a very

37

difficult day almost impossible. Let's just go through it, shall we? You started at eight o'clock in the morning with this extraordinary claim of yours that you didn't know we were going to America today. I'm sorry, Mark, but that means you're either terminally dense, or just not interested enough in your own family to register any information that isn't directly connected with hanging around the precinct with your dismal friends. You *must* have known we were going today – I think you *chose* not to know. And then, after coming out with all that rubbish, you disappear – goodness knows where – for hours and hours, leaving us to do all the work, then you stroll back in leaving the front door open – '

'*I* left the front door open this morning, Mummy,' said Felicity in a frightened, trying-to-make-things-better sort of voice.

'Ah, yes,' gritted Kathy, still addressing the back of Mark's head, 'but, you see, Felicity, when your dear brother does it, it's yet another symptom of the fact that anything that might benefit anyone else isn't even worth considering – totally irrelevant as far as you're concerned, isn't it, Mark?'

Mike leaned forward. 'Kath, don't you think you're going a bit over the – '

'Over the top? Is that what you were going to say?' Kathy was almost breathless with anger now. 'Yes, I am going over the top. I'm going over the top for good and sufficient reasons. I'm going over the top quite rationally, thank you very much, and if you must know I'm sick of the way you regard any attempt I make to discipline this – this *child* as some kind of neurotic outburst.'

Bending down and resting her forearms on the table, she spoke right into the side of Mark's face. He twitched his head slightly away from hers and went on eating. 'I find it utterly inconceivable that you can walk back into this house and sound put out because the rest of the family have decided to eat, instead of waiting for you to grace us with your presence at whatever time you see fit to come in.' She breathed deeply for a moment or two. 'Now, I'm going to tell you what I want. I want to know what you think about all the things I've just said – unless, of course, *you* think that I'm being unreasonable as well. *Is* that what you think?'

To my ears, the washing-machine-like noise of Mark's eating was amplified in the pause that followed, until it seemed to fill the kitchen and the house and the whole world. Seeing that he was lifting another mouthful to replace the one that was on the point of being swallowed, Kathy took hold of his wrist and repeated her question.

'*Do* you think I'm being unreasonable?'

I suppose that if a committee had been appointed at this stage in the proceedings, with the express purpose of devising the worst possible response for Mark to make to his mother, it might, after some weeks, or even months, of deliberation, have come up with something less politic than what he actually said, but I doubt it.

'Why can't I stay here and look after myself while you all go to America?'

That was what he actually said, and it was the straw that well and truly broke the camel's back. Kathy snatched the laden fork from Mark's hand and threw it across the table, where it landed in front of her oldest son, who had just finished his own lunch. Jack stretched an absent-minded hand out and then withdrew it again quickly, suddenly aware, I suppose, that such crude opportunism was inappropriate, to say the least.

'You stupid little . . . !' Kathy was almost beyond words now. Pulling Mark to his feet, she held him and shook him by both wrists, pushing her face right into his as she shouted. 'How can you say such stupid things? You stupid, stupid . . . ! Do you know how much this holiday is costing us? Do you know how long it's taken to plan? What the hell do you mean by asking if you can stay at home? I can't believe you could do this to us – the amount of money we've spent on you lately – you just don't care, do you? When you needed a lift to town yesterday to get your precious trainers the whole household screeched to a halt so that you could have what you wanted. But that means nothing, does it? The fact is you just don't care. You don't care! You don't care!'

Anger became tears again. Kathy was crying out from a place in her that had nothing to do with the present conflict. Some wound from the past had been opened, and it was hurting her. The trouble was, it was hurting Mark as well, in ways that confused and frightened him. With his face set hard against the torrent of emotion, he wrenched himself from his mother's grasp and spat words back at her in a strangely pitched pseudo-adult voice.

'Why do you say nasty things about my friends, then? An' why do you always talk about what you've done for me and how much money you've spent on me when you think I've done something wrong. *You're* the one who doesn't care!'

Turning abruptly, he stomped away along the hall and we heard his footsteps pounding up the stairs above our heads towards his bedroom. A door slammed violently and then there was silence.

Felicity said, 'Why is everything so horrible on our holiday day?' and burst into tears. Jack lifted her carefully onto his lap and put his arms round her.

Kathy didn't seem to be conscious of anything but her own response to Mark's parting shot. '*I'm* the one who doesn't care – I'm the one who doesn't care – I'm the one . . . ' Rage flowed in and out of her as if she was breathing it. 'I'll teach the little rat to slam doors!'

As she set off at a near sprint towards the stairs, Mike rose to his feet and called out nervously, 'Kath, don't you think you ought to wait until . . . ?' He subsided. Kathy wasn't about to take suggestions from anyone, let alone feebly expressed advice from her husband.

We waited and listened. Kathy's feet on the stairs sounded heavily above us just as Mark's had done, but then, unaccountably, there was complete silence – no crashes, no shouts, no screams, no explosions of any kind. Straining our ears for the slightest sound, we sat and said nothing for what seemed like a very long time, although it was probably only a couple of minutes.

'She's killed him', said Jack.

I found this remark less than amusing in the circumstances, but, despite the fact that tears still stood in her eyes, Felicity was obviously greatly relieved by what she saw as the total absurdity of Jack's comment. She giggled as though she'd been tickled. Mike expelled the breath he had been holding and let his chin drop to his chest like a weight suddenly released. 'I think,' he said, studying his interlocked fingers on the table as he spoke, 'it's probably going to be all right – for a while, anyway.' He stood up. 'I'll put some of this food in the oven for when Kath and Mark come down. I expect we all feel a bit – bruised at the moment, but it'll all be okay later on.'

'What time have you got to be at Heathrow, Mike?' I asked.

He closed the oven door and glanced over his shoulder at the clock. 'We need to check in by six, so if we're away from here by four-thirty we should be okay. Plenty of time if you really meant what you said about clearing up after us, Dip.'

'Oh, I meant what *I* said, Mike. How about you? Did you mean what you said?'

'Did I mean . . . ? Ah, well, all things being equal – and that's by no means guaranteed in this household, as you were well aware long before this last little domestic interlude – you're going to hear a bit more about that just before we leave, and I think you'll be surprised how much – '

Mike broke off as Kathy appeared in the door-way. Tears, anger and tension had all disap-peared. She looked quite happy, though somewhat sheepish.

'Hello, everybody,' she said, 'I've come to make huge acts of contrition. Felicity, darling, come and give Mummy a cuddle. I didn't mean to get cross with you like that.'

The little girl's unhesitating, scrambling descent from Jack's lap was a wonderful display of that un-conditional, joy-filled forgiveness with which some children freshen the world. She ran across the kitchen, threw herself into her mother's arms, and, after a long swinging hug, asked (as I rather thought she might) the question whose repetition proved that Felicity really did believe in her mother's apology.

'Mummy, why *don't* we say grace when it's just us, like they do at Emily's house?'

We all burst into laughter, including Kathy, who said, 'I'm afraid the answer's exactly the same even when I'm not cross, sweetheart. You're stuck with your silly old Mummy – '

'And your silly old Daddy', contributed Mike.

'Whereas lucky old Emily has a mummy and daddy who are nice and calm and organized and do all the right things at the right times, *even when no one's looking*! And good for them, I say. I wish I was like it, but I'm not.'

Felicity squeezed Kathy's cheeks with the thumb and forefinger of each hand, then drew back her head and chortled at her mother's distorted face. 'I *want* to be stuck with you and Daddy,' she said, putting on a very little girl's voice. 'I wouldn't want to be stuck with Emily's mummy.'

'Nor would I!' said Mike with unexpected passion, and everyone except Felicity laughed again.

'Did you kill Mark?' enquired Jack pleasantly.

'No, I didn't kill him, Jack – not this time. Please forgive me for sounding off at you the way I did just now. It wasn't you, although the milk bottles do make me cross. I shouldn't have gone on like that. I really am sorry.' She lowered Felicity to the floor and addressed Jack again. 'Would you mind making a start on taking the cases out to the van, love? And there are quite a lot of small bags as well, so Felicity can come and give you a hand. You'd like to do that for Mummy, wouldn't you, Felicity?'

Felicity looked at her mother with the narrowed eyes of an expert decoder. 'I want to stay and hear what happened with Mark as well', she said.

'Come on, Flitty.' Jack uncoiled himself from his chair and held out a hand. 'You know they won't talk about it while you're here, anyway, so we might as well go and do the bags. Tell you what – you can have a chocolate drop for every bag you take out. How's that?'

'You haven't got any chocolate drops', said Felicity, looking hopefully up into her brother's face.

'Oh, haven't I? How do you know I haven't got a packet hidden away in my room?'

''Cause I'd have found them by now if there were any.'

'Oh, you would, would you? Right – you've had it now!'

Frowning with mock severity Jack hoisted his giggling sister up onto his shoulder and marched away with her, closing the door between the kitchen and the rest of the house behind him with his foot. Squeals of anguish and ecstatic laughter floated back from the hall as the pair headed for the front sitting room.

'Is Mark coming down to finish his lunch?' asked Mike quietly.

Kathy nodded as she pulled a chair up to the table. 'Yes, he'll be here in a minute. I shan't want any food – not after eating all those words. I just wanted to tell you what happened upstairs.'

I was suddenly embarrassed. 'Would you like me to go and give Jack a hand? I don't mind at all . . . ' Feeling hot and heavy I made a movement as if to leave, but Kathy reached across and laid a restraining hand on my shoulder.

'You are joking, aren't you, Dip? If I'm not bothered about you seeing the worst of my dirty washing I'm certainly not going to mind you seeing one of the rare occasions when a scrap of underwear actually gets laundered, am I? In fact – I insist. Incidentally, that reminds me. We were going to suggest something for you to think about while we're in – '

'I've already mentioned it to Dip,' interrupted Mike, 'we'll say some more about that just before we go. Tell us what happened with Mark.'

'Oh, right . . . you've mentioned it, right.' Momentarily, Kathy searched my face for a response, but found none. The Robinsons may be good at having clean tea-towels, but I am very good at closing my face. Kathy knitted her brows in thought for a second, then spoke. 'About Mark – okay, well, I set off up the stairs with the deliberate intention of doing him some kind of serious physical damage. You probably guessed that, right?'

'We had an inkling', replied Mike solemnly.

'I went up there like an express train, and I wasn't thinking at all. I could only feel all these emotions crashing around inside me.' She waved a hand in the direction of her husband. 'Mike's seen it all many times, of course – been on the receiving end of it more than once as well, I'm afraid. I just get filled up with this wild, storming fear.'

'Fear of what, Kathy?'

'I'm not quite sure. The night, the end, everything falling apart, not being loved, some kind of looming final disaster – I don't really know. I've never been able to pin it down. It's always been there under the surface, waiting for something like this Mark business to open the cellar door and let it out. Don't get me wrong – Mark *has* been a pain in the neck, and he does need sorting out. He can be a little devil. The trouble is that after these dreadful feelings have been going on in me for a while they stop having anything to do with the thing or person that set them off. But it's too late by then – the express is going at full speed and someone usually gets hurt. You see, the problem is, Dip, I ain't got no brakes on my train.'

'But something stopped you this time.'

Kathy placed the palms of her hands together like a child in prayer, resting her face on the tips of her fingers as she considered. She looked up. 'Yes, it did. It was something I read this morning in the blighted fox-hole that we risibly refer to as our Quiet Time. It was the bit about loving our enemies. Jesus said we have to love our enemies. Mike and I decided we had one person each we'd describe as real "Enemies", didn't we, Mike?'

Mike frowned guiltily. 'Yes, we were going to pray for them, but unfortunately we got a bit err . . . distracted by thinking up all sorts of tortures we'd like to put them through – '

'You mean *I* did. Non-stop Scottish music in a confined space whilst playing Monopoly with our three children – that sort of thing.' Kathy grinned, enjoying the memory. 'Anyway, just now when I arrived upstairs and I was about to push the door in like an American detective and pull Mark's head off, I remembered those three words – Love Your Enemies. And I suddenly realized that – oh, Mike, it was awful – I realized that, in that moment, I was thinking of my *own son* as my enemy. I still wanted to kill him, you understand, but I was brought up short by . . . ' She brushed the hair back from her forehead. 'I was brought up short by the knowledge that I could either obey by loving him, whatever that might involve, or disobey by giving in to my own feelings. Standing outside that door, still seething away, it seemed as simple as that.'

'The Lord was speaking to you', said Mike, his eyes shining. 'That's what you've always wanted, Kath. Always happens to other people, but never to you – that's what you've said so many times.'

Exasperation shadowed Kathy's face. 'I wish you'd resist the temptation to turn the whole of life into an infant classroom, Mike. You can go around sticking helpful little labels on all your experiences if you like, but I'd like mine left as they are, thank you very much. Maybe God *was* talking to me. I don't know. All I know for sure is that I thought and felt certain things, and that, as a result, I did things differently – that's all.'

'Sorry, Kath', said Mike. His tone was repentant, but his eyes were still shining.

'What did you do in the end, Kathy?'

'In the end, Dip, I turned the handle of the door very, very slowly with that intensive muscular control you use when you're in a temper but you don't want it to show, and walked in. Mark had actually got into bed in his clothes – he knows I hate him doing that during the day – and he was sitting up reading a comic. He was obviously waiting for the explosion, as I'm sure you all were down here. I sat down on his bed without saying anything and he looked at me a bit puzzled before pretending to go back to his comic. Then I put my arms out and said, "I love you, Mark – whatever happens in the next five minutes, I'll always love you – whatever happens." He lowered the comic and looked at me for a second, then he put his arms out and we had a cuddle. He said something like "Sorry I've been a bit off, Mum" and I said "I'm sorry I've been a bit off as well", and that was it really. He's coming down to have his lunch in a minute, so . . . ' She broke off and then gave a little laugh.

'What were you thinking then, Kath?' said Mike.

'Just – how pathetic I am,' replied Kathy, 'a bit of affection – that's all I need to chase the cold away. A good hug, and the sun comes out. I'm such a child. All my troubles seem to resolve themselves into one big question. Do you still love me? I tell you what, though,' she added with a smile, 'it's a good job he did respond, because if he hadn't – I'd have thrown him through the window.'

Peace reigned for some time after that. Mark duly appeared, apparently unaffected by the recent trauma, ate his own and his mother's share of the remaining food, and talked to me with transparently genuine happiness about the family adventure that was about to begin. When I asked him if he had really not known that the holiday was to start today he insisted that he had thought it was next Saturday, and went on to explain at some length that he had only been upset because he and his friends had planned to go fishing on the Monday, and he'd been 'well looking forward to that' because they were going to take sandwiches and drinks and (quite inexplicably to me) a football, and they were coming back to Mark's house in the evening to cook and eat all the fish that would have been caught during the day, and it had to be Mark's house because none of his friends' mothers liked a mess in their kitchens. I stored up this last, slightly backhanded, compliment to pass on to Kathy at an appropriate time in the future.

By four-fifteen the Robinsons were ready to go. Felicity, full of excitement and chocolate drops, skipped up and down the hall singing, 'We're going to

America!' over and over again, until, together with her two brothers, she was summoned by her father for a last-minute family conference around the kitchen table. Mike sat at the end nearest the window, looking a little nervous as he waited for the hubbub to subside. I was feeling nervous too. I suddenly regretted my earlier move into self-revelation and wished that everything could stay exactly the way it had always been, for ever.

'Isn't it funny,' said Kathy, when the general chatter had died down,' how you feel just before you go off on a trip like this? You've been looking forward to it for ages, you've been ever so excited about going, it's what you really want, and yet – I can't describe it exactly – at this precise moment I'd like to settle down amongst all these nice familiar, safe things and just be at home. Does that sound very silly?'

'Yes,' said Felicity simply, 'very silly indeed, Mummy.' She gave a little rippling laugh at the thought of such foolishness. 'Of course we don't want to stay here. We want to go to America.' She turned to her father. 'Is America in England, Daddy?'

'No, darling,' replied Mike, sounding slightly shocked at this vast gap in his daughter's geographical compehension, 'you *know* it isn't. I've explained to you that we have to go in a big aeroplane across an enormous sea called the Atlantic Ocean because America is a completely different country. I showed you on the map, remember?'

'It's where the cowboys and Indians come from, Flitty,' added Jack, 'like on telly.'

'I thought it was where Disneyland is.' There was a trace of anxiety in Felicity's voice as she tried to make sense of her six-year-old store of information. 'We're going there, aren't we, Mummy?'

'Of course we are,' said Kathy reassuringly, 'it's going to be such fun.'

'There aren't any cowboys and Indians any more, Flit,' explained Mark, 'they all dress like us in America now and they don't wear guns.'

'Joke!' Jack leaned his chair back on two legs and guffawed loudly.

Mark's face hardened angrily. 'Why is what I say a joke? Why wasn't what you said a joke?'

'There may not be any cowboys and Indians any more, but to say that Americans don't have guns nowadays is plain ridiculous. There are more guns per person in the United States of America than in any other – '

'I never said they don't have guns any more. I said they don't *wear* them like they used to. You never listen to what anyone else says, that's your trouble. You're too busy pretending to be grown-up, and listening to music that nobody else understands because it's so bad that they can't be bothered.'

'Oh, get lost!' Jack turned his face away from Mark. 'I hope he's not going to be like this for the next three weeks. I don't know if I can stand it.'

Jack's languid dismissiveness detonated something in Mark. 'Why don't you shut up, Jack! You make me sick! You make me – '

'Mummy, there *are* still cowboys and Indians in America.' Something had risen to the surface of

Felicity's memory. 'I've seen them in a thing on television about Disneyland. They've *got* them at Disneyland. Jack and Mark both said that there aren't any any more, but there are, aren't there?'

Mark had folded his arms as if to contain the furies that occupied him. He spoke in terse, clipped tones. 'Dad, can I not sit next to Jack on the plane, please?'

'Suits me,' drawled Jack, 'I don't want to sit next to a silly little boy for hours and hours.'

Kathy put both hands over her ears. 'If you two don't – '

'Mummy, tell Mark and Jack that there are still cowboys and Indians in America. They both said – '

'Stop.' Mike didn't raise his voice at all, but there was something about the firmness of intention behind his one word that secured everyone's attention. 'I'm afraid we're all being rather selfish. This last little bit was supposed to be for Dip. It wasn't supposed to be an opportunity for Jack and Mark to see how unpleasant they could be to each other. I'd like you both to say sorry to her, please.'

There are few things more excruciating than having to receive apologies from people who have been instructed to offer them, but I couldn't help smiling as both of the boys mumbled their penitence.

So difficult, I thought, for Jack, poised between childhood and growing-up, to find the stability to cope with older *and* younger folk. Felicity was too little to present a problem – indeed, I sensed that she made him feel more like an adult, but Mark must be a significant image in the juvenile picture of himself that Jack didn't want to acknowledge any more. Scorn and dismissiveness seemed to be the only weapons he had found to use in the battle to prevent his younger brother dragging him back into a world that he yearned to leave behind.

Perhaps it was even more difficult for Mark to understand why the big brother who had probably been closer to him than anyone else for the last few years, was becoming so treacherously distant in manner and lifestyle. I felt such sympathy for both of them.

'Did I do anything wrong, Daddy?' asked Felicity interestedly.

'Not quite,' said Mike, smiling despite himself, 'but you can apologize to Dip as well if you like. That'll count for the next time you do something naughty.'

This idea appealed enormously to Felicity. Kneeling on her chair she draped her arms around my neck and rested her head on my shoulder. 'Oh, Dip,' she cried theatrically, 'please forgive me for the next naughty thing I do. I can't tell you how sorry I shall be!'

I patted Felicity's back. 'Thank you very much, Felicity, I shall look forward to that. Actually – I think Mike's the only member of this family who hasn't apologized to me today. I'm beginning to wish I could do something bad myself, then I'd be able to apologize to one of you.'

Mike clapped his hands briskly three times. 'Right! No more messing about. No more arguing. Let's show Dip what we've done. Can you get out that certain something we made yesterday, please, Mark?'

'Oh, yeah!' Mark's eyes came alight with anticipation as he stood up and reached into the lower cupboard of the kitchen dresser that stood beside the back door. Releasing me from her embrace, Felicity bounced her bottom up and down on her ankles and flapped her hands with excitement.

'This is the surprise, Dip!' she squealed, 'I did some of it. You look!'

'Take the other end, Jack,' said Kathy, 'he can't manage it on his own. You two may not agree about most things, but I know you feel the same about this.'

'Okay, Mum. Close your eyes until we tell you, Dip.' Jack rose amicably to his feet and took one end of the long, concertinaed strip of paper that Mark had been carefully unfolding.

I closed my eyes.

When the chorus of 'Look now!' came, I opened my eyes to see an eight-foot paper banner, decorated with stars and trees and people and all sorts of less identifiable shapes in every colour of the felt-pen rainbow. It was a beautiful piece of work, but most beautiful of all was the message spelt out in capital letters that had been cut from coloured paper and stuck on separately:

WE LOVE YOU DIP –
COME AND LIVE WITH US

When I was a young girl at school in Adelaide I wrote a story which included the immortal words – 'Two pairs of eyes stared at him open-mouthed . . . '. I seem to remember that my English teacher was not at all impressed by this unintentional flight of anatomical fantasy. She spent some time trying to explain that eyes don't have mouths and therefore cannot open them, but, perhaps because we focused on it for so long, that incorrect phrase has stuck in my mind ever since. Every time someone looks at me in a certain way I say to myself, 'That pair of eyes is looking at me open-mouthed'. That's how it was in the kitchen now. Five pairs of Robinson eyes were staring at me open-mouthed, and I knew that five pairs of Robinson ears were waiting for me to respond in the most obvious way, by simply saying, 'Yes, of course I'll come and live with you'.

It would have been so easy to say exactly that – not immediately, because my eyes filled with tears and I had to hunt for a tissue in my sleeves – but once I'd recovered I could have said the words, and that would have been that. I'm very grateful to God for that little pause, because I think it saved me from making a serious mistake.

'Dip,' I felt Felicity's arm creep around my shoulders, 'if you come to live with us, you'll be able to tell me lots more stories about crocodiles and jellyfish and things, and you could take turns with Mummy and Daddy putting me to bed.'

This ingenuous assessment of the major benefits likely to accrue to me if I moved in with the Robinsons made me laugh but also set the tears flowing again for some reason.

'We all mean it', said Mark gruffly. 'Flit an' me

did the colouring an' Jack did the letters. We spent ages on it.'

'Please forgive me, everybody,' I said damply, dabbing my eyes as I spoke, 'it was such a lovely surprise that it made me cry. I'm sorry to be so silly – it really is the most beautiful thing I've ever seen, and you must have worked so hard on it.' I gave Felicity a quick squeeze. 'Thank you, darling – and Mark and Jack. When you've gone I'm going to have a really good look at all those pictures. I can't tell you what it means to know that you took all that trouble, and that you – you love me enough to want me living in your house. It makes me feel very special.'

Kathy slid the palms of her hands from side to side across the table-top, as if sweeping away invisible obstacles. 'So, what's the answer, Dip? Yes or no?'

'No, Kath, don't bully – we said we'd leave Dip to think about it while we're in America, and that's what we're going to do.' Mike turned to me. 'Kath and I didn't do any of the banner, Dip, but we mean it just as much as the others. We'd love you to live here, but it's up to you. Let us know what you've decided when we come back. It's not something you can decide on the spot. Now!' He peered at the clock. 'If we don't go in the next few minutes we're going to be in trouble. You boys fold the banner up and leave it on the table. You know about the keys and the switches and everything, don't you Dip? It's all yours till we get back.' He looked from face to face. 'Anything else?'

Felicity prodded an accusing finger into my chest. 'You've been saying for ages and ages that you'd tell me why you're called "Dip" before we went to America. Now you've got to. Why are you?'

I have never really understood why I desperately hang on to secrets that would seem foolish and trivial to anyone else. Perhaps it's something to do with living alone in your own little world for so long. I had put Felicity off again and again, without knowing quite why, but now the deadline I had so rashly specified was upon me and there was no escape.

'I'll tell you very quickly,' I replied, 'because you've got to go, so listen carefully.'

Felicity nodded, eyes huge with interest. I took a deep breath.

'When I was a little girl I used to play with my cousin called James, who was a bit older than me, but very nice.'

'I've got three cousins,' said Felicity proudly, 'and they're called Paul, Rachel and Amy. They're very perfect and they live in West Wickham.'

'Well, I only had this one called James, who wasn't perfect, and he lived in a place called Glenelg, which was near the sea.'

'In Australia?'

'In Australia, yes. My mummy and I used to travel on a funny old thing that was a bit like a train and a bit like a tram – I loved going on it – from Adelaide, which was the big city where we lived when I was small, to Glenelg, where James lived with his mummy and daddy and a much older brother. One morning we went to see them when it had been raining through the night, and we all went shopping together. The sun had come out and it was very hot, but there were puddles everywhere, and because my mummy had made me wear my rubber boots I was allowed to jump around in them as much as I liked. James wasn't, because he had his best shoes on – I don't think he was very pleased really. Anyway, when we stopped somewhere for the grown-ups to have a cup of tea and us to have an ice-cream, James told me that he'd been reading a book about red Indians – '

'Like I'll see in Disneyland?'

'Yes, that's right, and this book said that little Red Indian children were given their names when they were older than children in Australia or England, because their mummies and daddies wanted to see what they were like, and call them something that really suited them. So, for example, let's say you liked to practise a lot with a toy bow and arrow, well, your name might end up as "Hunts With Arrows", or if your favourite game was pretending to be a galloping pony you might be called "Running Horse". James said that if I was a little Red Indian girl who hadn't got a name yet my mummy would have to call me "Dances In Puddles". I was very cross with James for saying that, but my mummy, and James' mummy and daddy and big brother laughed and laughed and laughed, and when we were back in Adelaide my mummy told the story to lots of people we knew. Then someone noticed that the first letters of "Dances In Puddles" made DIP, and they said that's what I should be called. So "Dip" has been my name ever since.'

There is no history of anyone except Felicity

expressing any great enthusiasm for my narrative talents, so I was a little taken aback to discover, on looking around the table, that every member of the Robinson clan appeared totally transfixed by the true story I had just told.

'Go on,' I said, breaking the spell. 'Go! You'll miss your plane. Go to America!'

Two minutes later they were all packed into the van ready to leave, and I was leaning on Felicity's pillar, waiting to wave goodbye. Through an open side-window I distinctly heard Mark making the provocative suggestion that, if Jack had been a Red Indian, he would have been known as 'Listens To Rubbish'. I wondered how harmonious the journey was likely to be. Finally, with much wild hand-waving and loud shouts of farewell, the Robinsons were gone.

I watched the van disappear over the brow of Maiden Hill, then I lingered for a moment, enjoying the afternoon sunshine, and talked very quietly to God about the Robinsons.

'Father,' I said, 'you gave me a wonderful gift today, and I'm really grateful. Ever since we first met I've been asking you for someone special to love me. You've given me a whole family, and I'm really pleased. Don't cancel the order for the Paul Newman look-alike, I'm still in the market for that, whatever I might say about personal space – but I'm so pleased they want me.' Tears filled my eyes again suddenly. 'Look after those Robinsons, Lord, and help them not to be too disappointed when I tell them I can't come and live with them, because I don't think I can – not yet.'

Chapter Four

I did enjoy being left in charge of the Robinsons' home, not so much because of the chance to sift through everyone's private papers and Mike's fabled pornography, but because there simply is something very 'tasty' about roaming freely in somebody else's house when there's absolutely no chance of them coming back.

As I finished my prayer by the gate-post and walked back inside I felt oddly light-headed, as though I'd had just the right amount to drink. The front door shut behind me with one of those very satisfactory locked-on-the-inside sounds, and I paused in the hall for a moment, savouring the very particular hush that falls over a newly de-familied house.

In the kitchen I made myself a coffee exactly the way *I* liked it for once – weak, with just a suggestion of sugar – and sat on a stool by the open window overlooking the garden.

I knew that I was going to have to work through my feelings about the invitation I'd just had, and I also wanted to be very clear in my own mind about the best way to tell the family that I didn't yet feel able to move in with them, but I couldn't face all that just now. Maybe it would be easier just to forget my reservations and do what they wanted. The cowardly way out was very tempting at that moment. I sighed.

Such heavy considerations would have to be post-poned while I had a little board meeting with myself concerning my immediate responsibilities as guardian of the Robinson castle.

These meetings with myself tend to be fairly lively, because when I'm on my own I chatter to myself, a habit which, if I'm not careful, can sometimes leak out into places where other people are likely to be. More than once I've turned the corner of a street, haranguing myself quite loudly and sternly on some topic, only to be confronted by an alarmed member of the public coming in the other direction who, quite reasonably, was expecting to encounter at least two people, if not a large public meeting. There is only one feeble thing that I have ever been able to think of doing in that situation – I sing, and try to give the impression that that's what I was doing all along. Pathetic, isn't it?

I felt I was quite safe in the Robinsons' kitchen.

'Right,' I said out loud to myself, 'living creatures first. Just the two stick-insects to be fed and tickled. Thank goodness Stan is no more.'

Until recently, Felicity had owned an obnoxiously bad-tempered hamster, christened 'Stan' by Kathy, because the expression on his beady-eyed little face as he sniffed with incredulous disdain at food, people, the air and everything else, bore an uncanny resemblance to the expression habitually worn by one of our older church members. Every attempt to handle him and establish friendly relations – with the hamster, that is, not the church member – had been met with such energetically relentless biting and weeing, that even Felicity's enthusiasm waned after a time, and Stan, presumably enraged at being deprived of the opportunity to inflict pain and dampness, became a sort of Houdini of the hamster world. Despite being confined in an extravaganza of purpose-built, brightly coloured plastic tubes and living spaces, described in true American style on the side of the box it came in as a 'Small Animal Module', he discovered that, given time, he could always find a way to nibble himself to freedom. He would make triumphant appearances on the kitchen work-surface or the window-sill, sniffing smugly and daring his human jailers to re-incarcerate him. The queue for this task was never a very long one and it trickled away to nothing as the weeks went by. Whenever the cry went up 'Stan's out!' all Robinsons (and one Reynolds if I was visiting at the time) would suddenly discover pressing engagements elsewhere, and Stan would be left to feel, with some justification, that he had possessed the land – well, the kitchen anyway.

It was usually Kathy who ended up sacrificing flesh and dryness to get the animal back into its cage, although truth compels me to admit that she generally performed this task with a conspicuous lack of Christian grace and goodwill – not that anyone blamed her for that. We were too relieved that she was doing it to worry much about the spirit in which it was done. Mike attempted to intervene only once. I recall the occasion well.

There had been such a sound of crashing, and such a torrent of swearing, snarling abuse issuing from the kitchen where Kathy was dealing with Stan, that it seemed to those of us crouched in hiding (Felicity and I) as if she must be rolling over and over on the floor with the creature, locked in mortal combat. Mike, who simply cannot leave well alone at times, abandoned the television programme he'd been watching in the sitting room, and took up a position in the kitchen doorway from which he remonstrated mildly but firmly with his wife over the language she was using.

I don't know if Kathy actually threw Stan at Mike, or what happened at the end of that particular row, because, at this juncture, Felicity and I folded our tents and stole quietly away to play on the swings at the recreation ground, but I do know that (to my knowledge) Mike never criticized any aspect of Kathy's Stan-handling again. A few weeks after that incident God had mercy on the afflicted. He caused Stan to escape captivity in the middle of the night, and the small but powerful creature was never seen again by any of us. Felicity was encouraged to believe that he was well and happy in some Promised Land behind the wainscoting, but I think the rest of us felt fairly sure that biting, weeing Stan had gone to that great Small Animal Module in the sky, and, to be honest, we were glad – although we felt very sorry for the angel who would have to look after him.

Stan's departure meant that my sole living charges for the next few weeks were the stick-insects, which belonged to Mark, nominally at any rate, and they had certainly never caused any direct harm to anyone. Being of a type that is native to Australia, they had originally (and terribly unoriginally) been given the names Bruce and Sheila, but at my suggestion had been rechristened Rowan and Kimberley, names that were equally Australian in flavour but a little less crudely predictable. Now, as I sipped my coffee and leaned down to tickle Kimberley's tummy with my thumbnail, I couldn't help smiling as I recalled the events surrounding their arrival in the Robinson household.

Mark had brought them home one Friday evening after a school trip which included a visit to a nature centre on the South Downs. He demonstrated a certain gruff pride in relaying the information he had been given by the person who had sold him the insects. Mike and Kathy were obviously (and understandably) more than happy to cancel their statutorily annoyed response to the fact that Mark had spent some of his emergency outing money without permission. In Mark's case enthusiasm and voluntary communication were too rare to be squandered on recrimination.

'She said they're an Australian sort,' he explained, 'and one's male and one's female, and they'll get really big, and one'll have wings but I can't remember if it's the male or the female, and they only eat bramble leaves, and you have to spray 'em with water instead of giving 'em it in a pot or something, and if we want to know anything else it's all right to phone them at the place, because they always like to know what's happened to their stick-insects.'

The next day, inspired by the interest that Mark had shown in his new pets, Mike decided to construct a specially designed home for Rowan and Kimberley out of an old bedside-unit drawer while the boy was out. I must say, speaking as a total incompetent in the field of 'making things', that I was very impressed.

First of all he cut a piece out of the bottom of the drawer and made it into a removable hatch, held on by a groove at one end and a piece of wood that rotated on a nail at the other. Then he carefully shaped another, larger piece of wood so that it would hold a small glass bottle which could be filled with water and used to keep the bramble leaves fresh. This piece of wood was glued and nailed into place so that the bottle would be vertical when the drawer was standing up on end. Finally, he pinned a sheet of fine gauze across the top of the drawer, and stood the whole thing upright so that the original handle of the drawer was on top, and could be used to lift Rowan and Kimberley's new world from one place to another. It was brilliant!

People who can do that sort of thing have difficulty understanding people who can't. As Mike worked methodically away on a table out in the sunny little brick-paved yard at the back of the house, I sat on the doorstep watching the whole process, and was quite fascinated. I found myself wishing yet again that I was able to use practical skills with such confidence.

'How do you know what to do next?' I asked Mike when the thing was finished. 'I mean – an hour ago you didn't have a stick-insect cage, and now you have got one. You just *did* it, as though you'd got grade one at "A" level in making stick-insect cages. Who told you how to do it? What made you think of using the drawer in the first place? And then there's this little thing you've made to put the bottle in – I mean, it's so clever. Why can't I do things like that? I would have made some holes in a cardboard box, dropped a few leaves in, and that would have been that. But this – well, it's a mansion!'

Mike laughed at the escalating mania that I deliberately injected into my speech, but, like nearly all the practical people I've ever known, he didn't really understand what I was talking about. He shrugged and gestured with his competent hands.

'I just think about what's needed and then – well, I just do it I suppose. Bit by bit, stage by stage, that's the way my mind works. You could have done this, Dip. You must do all sorts of things on the wards. It's only a couple of bits of wood and a scrap of gauze. Anyone could have done it – honestly.'

Mmmm . . .

The cage was duly presented to Mark when he came in later, and he was just as impressed as I had been.

'Thanks Dad, that's great!' he enthused. 'Shall I put 'em in now?'

The rest of the family gathered in the yard and watched as Mark removed Rowan and Kimberley from the small plastic pot covered in perforated cling-film that had been their home since yesterday, and installed them in their smart new residence, freshly stocked with the best bramble leaves that my, now slightly scratched, hands had been able to pick a little earlier. I couldn't honestly say that my two fellow antipodeans registered any discernible joy or amazement at this unexpected move from bed-sitter to Buckingham Palace, but I have no doubt that, on some deep entomological level, they knew the good times had come. Felicity put her face up close to the gauze and peered with intent excitement at the motionless inhabitants of the cage.

'I'm going to watch them till they move', she said, more to herself than anyone else.

'Have we got the spray for the water yet?'

That was Mark's question, and it turned this pleasant little occasion into a typically Robinsonian family argument. It was one of the first ones that I'd witnessed, and it was an absolute classic, demonstrating the way in which full-blown conflict could begin with an issue so trivial that, later, no one was able to remember what it had been.

'Oh, I don't think we need to specially buy a spray,' replied Mike mildly, 'just stick your hand under the cold tap and then sort of shake it in their direction, that's all they'll need.'

Like many people who respond negatively towards authority in one arena, Mark could be extraordinarily literal when it came to carrying out the instructions and recommendations of anyone whose authority he *had* decided to accept.

'No, the lady at the place said it had to be a spray so it goes over them fine, and not splashing big drops.'

Mike scratched his head. 'I take your point, Mark, but there isn't really going to be any difference, is there? You don't have to drown them just because you do it with your hand. Just make sure you do it from a distance and it'll be exactly the same as using a spray. After all, the stick-insects won't know whether it's a spray or not, will they?'

'I don't care – she said use a spray', said Mark sullenly, his mouth tightening with determination. 'They're my stick-insects an' I'll do what I like.'

'The stick-insects *might* know the difference, you know, Dad', contributed Jack in his best provocative manner. 'Kimberley will say, "Rowan, old chap, are you altogether happy with the way in which our water is being served at the moment? I mean – does this Mark Thingummybob honestly think we're prepared to be fobbed off with random-sized globules of water that he just happens to fling in our direction? Why, yesterday I was hit by what I can only describe as a Big Drop. I don't know about you, but I positively refuse to drink any more water unless it comes out of a spray. After all, this Mark person must have heard what The Lady said".'

Mark turned on Jack. 'Why don't you mind your own business, beanpole features? I never asked you to come an' watch anyway. Why don't you go an' pretend to read something clever or something. No one wants you here!'

Kathy, inflammable as ever, turned on Mark. 'Excuse me, Mark, but I *do* want Jack here if it's all the same to you, and I also want to point out that when you say these animals belong to you, you are in fact completely wrong.' She rested a knuckle on the corner of the table and placed her other hand on her hip. 'They were bought, if you'll just cast your mind back, with money that belonged to your father and me, money that you were supposed to bring home with you unless an emergency happened. We didn't say anything because we didn't want to make you unhappy . . . '

Kathy!

'Well, you have 'em, then,' grumped Mark, backing away until he was stopped short by the wall of the house, 'I don't want them any more. You have 'em if you're that worried about the stupid money!'

Jack put both hands flat on top of his head and swivelled the upper part of his body from side to side in disbelief. '*Why* do you have to be so childish, Mark? Do you realize Dad's spent most of the morning putting this thing together for you? Doesn't that count for – '

'Oh, come on now, everyone,' said Mike coaxingly, 'let's not get this whole thing out of perspective. The money's not really important, and it actually only took about an hour to do the cage. It would be a shame if – '

Kathy rotated ominously on her knuckle in Mike's direction. 'Oh, thanks! Thanks a bundle for supporting me, I *don't* think. I point out that he shouldn't have spent the money in the first place, and you tell him that the money's not important.' She swung both arms as if conducting a piece of music that she hated. 'I wish you didn't find it necessary to just dismiss what I say as if it can't possibly mean anything. If you think you can bring him up properly by apologizing to him every time *he* does something wrong, well – good luck to you, that's all I can say.'

Jack was sulking slightly under his tented hands. 'I was only trying to help, Dad. I just meant that you'd spent a long time making a house for his stick-insects, and it didn't seem fair – '

'Yeah, very helpful of you takin' the mickey out of me. Thanks a lot, Jack!'

Mike nodded. 'Well, I happen to think Mark is quite right this time, Jack. I'm grateful for your support, but – '

Kathy jumped on that. 'And I'd be grateful for yours if ever there was any – '

'Could I make a suggestion?'

There was a blessed hush as all eyes turned to me – all eyes, that is, except Felicity's. Seemingly unmoved by this particular pitched battle, she was still leaning on the table, concentrating hard on Rowan and Kimberley, apparently determined that when they did make their first move she would be the one to see it.

'Do forgive us, Dip,' said Kathy eventually, 'it's terribly bad manners to bite great lumps out of each other in front of visitors.'

There was a general, vaguely apologetic mumble.

'No, no, please don't apologize, and *please* whatever you do, don't sentence me to your good manners for the rest of my life. I really couldn't stand it. No, what I was going to say was – I mean, it's none of my business – '

Jack interrupted, sternly admonitory. 'Now, now, Dip, it's very bad manners to tell people that you don't want their good manners after they've just demonstrated their bad manners, and then to use

70

good manners yourself when they'd rather you used bad manners with them. Don't you agree?'

I laughed. 'Sorry, forgive my politeness, and my bad manners – what I was going to ask was whether I could make a suggestion that might help.'

There was a pause.

'Well – yes,' Mike glanced around a little uncertainly at the other members of his family, 'I'm sure we'd all be glad to try anything that might make things more peaceful, wouldn't we, everybody?'

Jack and Kathy nodded, Felicity didn't hear and Mark grunted something monosyllabic that might possibly have meant he would be glad to try anything that might make things more peaceful, but might quite easily have meant the exact opposite.

I ploughed ahead. 'Well, you remember how the argument started, don't you?'

They looked blankly at each other. I looked at them and said nothing for a moment. It was hard to believe that the origins of such a pungent exchange could be so easily forgotten. Surprisingly, it was Mark who hazarded the first guess.

'Was it about me spendin' the money on the stick-insects when I wasn't s'posed to?'

'Nnno,' I answered, sounding like a junior teacher who's just asked her class one of those very focused questions, 'no, that was mentioned, but it wasn't what actually started the row, was it?'

'Wait a minute,' said Mike, a little exasperated with himself, 'let's just work backwards. Mark said something about Jack taking the mickey out of him, because Jack had just said that I'd worked on the cage all morning and it wasn't fair because – ' Mike held his head with both hands and screwed his eyes tight shut – 'What was it that wasn't fair? It wasn't fair because . . . ?' He opened his eyes and extended both arms with open palms, inviting someone to fill in the missing information.

'Because Mark said he didn't want the stick-insects any more?' suggested Jack.

Mike clicked his fingers. 'That's right! Because he didn't want the stick-insects any more.' His face cleared. 'That's it!' His brow furrowed again. 'But why didn't he want the stick-insects any more?'

Everyone looked at Mark, who stared, open-mouthed with concentration, for several seconds before saying, 'Can't remember.'

Mike turned to Kathy, looking more perplexed than ever. 'And there was that bit in the middle somewhere, when you said something about me dismissing everything you say because it doesn't mean anything. What was that all about?'

Kathy's lips twitched silently as she thought. 'I think,' she said doubtfully, 'it was about the money that Mark spent – '

'Ah!' exclaimed Mike, 'so Mark was right. It *did* begin with the money.'

Kathy shook her head slowly. 'No, because I wasn't going to say anything about the money. There must have been some reason why I suddenly brought it up.'

'Because I told Jack no one wanted him here?' volunteered Mark.

It was becoming like a party game.

'That's it!' cried Kathy excitedly. 'And the reason you said that was because you didn't like Jack taking the mickey out of you about, err . . . something or other.'

They all exchanged blank looks again. Nobody seemed able to identify the mysterious Something Or Other.

'How to put the water in', said Felicity calmly and unexpectedly, without taking her eyes from the inside of the cage.

There was an instant of silent paralysis followed by hubbub.

'Of course!'

'Oh, yes!'

'About the water spray . . . '

'That was it!'

The commotion died away at last, and in the quiet that followed a single voice was heard. It was Mark's voice, and it said, 'When are we getting the spray for the water?'

I intervened hurriedly. 'Just before you have exactly the same argument all over again, here's what I was going to suggest. Mark, have you got the number of the place where you bought Rowan and Kimberley?'

'What, you mean the nature place?'

'Yes, the lady said you could phone whenever you need to know anything, didn't she?'

'How'd you know that?' Mark looked at me as if I'd done some amazing mind-reading trick.

I laughed. 'You told us when you first got them, you

ninny. Doesn't anyone in this family ever remember anything they've said? Listen, why don't you give her a ring and just ask if it has to be a spray or not? Then you'll know.'

Mark fished in his pocket and drew out a crumpled leaflet. He studied it for a moment.

'This is it,' he said, 'it's on the bottom at the back.' He looked up at me. 'You mean phone now?'

'Yes, go on.'

'All right – will you come with me, Jack?'

'Come on, then, I'll phone and you listen on the extension.'

The most sacred moments are miniscule and easily missed, are they not? Mark's request for help from his older brother in this ostensibly trivial little matter, and Jack's immediately positive response was a case in point. The two brothers were in continuous conflict mode at present, but something in Mark's vulnerability had drawn instinctive care from Jack, and in that small incident it was perhaps possible to see that the relationship they had once had was alive and well – if postponed – and would probably reassert itself in the future, when both boys had sorted out who and what they were.

To nobody's surprise, Mark and Jack returned a few minutes later with the news that it was not necessary to use a spray, as long as some moistness was introduced into the living environment from time to time.

'She said I could use a wet cloth,' said Mark, 'and sort of shake it over 'em.'

'Well, that's what I said in the first place,' replied

Mike, clapping his hand to his forehead, 'just wet your hand under the tap.'

'No, it has to be a cloth. She said – '

'They're moving, Mark!' squealed Felicity suddenly, 'Rowan and Kimberley are moving! I saw it first, didn't I?'

It was true. Six human heads crowded around the cage to watch as, very slowly, like two little pieces of mobile hay, Rowan and Kimberley began to investigate their bramble leaves, hoping, no doubt, that in due course, when the discussion had finished, some moistness would be introduced into their living environment. Whether this was to be effected by a specially bought spray, by a hand that had been held under a running tap, or by the shaking of a sacred wet cloth was not, I suspected, an issue that occupied a great deal of their time or attention.

I finished my coffee and put the mug in the sink to wash up later. Getting down from the stool I knelt and put my face up close to the front of the converted drawer, just as Felicity had done all those months ago, marvelling, as I did so, at the change in Rowan and Kimberley since the day when they arrived.

Mark's information about the stick-insects becoming really big had turned out to be quite accurate. The wispy little things from the plastic pot had grown to three or four inches in length and were about half an inch wide at the thickest part of their bodies. You could actually see their jaws moving nowadays when they consumed their beloved bramble leaves, and the larger one especially seemed to greatly enjoy being gently tickled as it clung to the gauze on the front of its cage. Some visitors found them repulsive, reckoning that the female in particular looked like a cross between a scorpion and a praying mantis, but I was rather fond of them, and perpetually intrigued by the fact that they were *made* of leaves.

'Don't worry,' I said to them, 'I'll make sure the grub keeps coming – after all, we ozzies have got to stick together, right?'

Having unearthed a pair of scissors from the drawer of the dresser, I wandered out into the garden to hunt for bramble leaves in the little wilderness area down behind the shed. Still in a rather light-headed mood, I paused dreamily in the centre of the lawn, enjoying an unusually warm April sun on my face, and reflected on the fact that one of my most persistent fantasies takes place in a garden, a garden, however, that boasts a little more style than the Robinsons' rather unmanicured third of an acre.

My dream garden, which fronts a magnificent mansion, is huge and ornate, featuring trim lawns, an occasional peacock (not the sandwich stealing variety), fountains and lakes, weather-beaten statues of shy maidens and chubby little boys, and, crucially, one of those really well-maintained mazes with the thick box hedges, with a sundial ringed by seats at the very centre.

In my fantasy I am wandering slowly (but fascinatingly) through this Chatsworth-type garden on a glitteringly dew-bedecked morning. I am afflicted with some deep and dramatic sadness, the sort that makes your eyes look bigger and more beautiful because they sparkle with unshed tears, and definitely not the sort where they look red and puffy and awful because you've been bawling like a baby. I think I'm usually wearing one of those full-length, old-fashioned dresses that has at least half a chance of disguising the matronly figure against which I have battled unsuccessfully for many years. My hair has grown mysteriously longer and more lustrous, and is firmly in the 'can't-stop-myself-from-running-my-hands-through-it' sort of bracket.

Eventually, after a decent period of wandering fascinatingly about, I become aware that I am being watched from the terrace of the mansion by a man who, oddly enough, combines every attractive feature that has ever appealed to me in the opposite sex. He is in his mid-thirties, tall and slim – but not thin – with well-set shoulders and a general air of physical alertness and strength. His hair is dark (or light if he looks like Paul Newman) and quite straight with a little curl at the point where it touches the collar. His face is mobile and sensitive, the large, honest eyes glimmering softly like deep pools in the moonlight (I would imagine), with just a hint of something wild and untamable beneath the surface. The blatantly expensive, tailor-made thirties-style suit is worn with casual elegance, and is obviously just one of many that he might select to throw on each morning.

Eventually this wonderful man detaches himself from the terrace wall he has been leaning on, de-scends the steps to the lawn and walks (with the obligatory lithe grace of a panther) slowly across the grass towards me. When we meet nothing is said. As I gaze into his eyes I sense that he too is suffering the pain of some terrible loss or tragedy (this is pretty good sensing on my part, when you consider that I still haven't got the faintest idea what's the matter with me, let alone him). We turn and, in silent communion, walk side by side through the nearby entrance to the maze (assuming it's wide enough) agreeing, without the need for mere vulgar words, that, in a very real sense, we shall be happier if we can be together in the midst of the puzzle that is life. (Occasionally I wonder if I ought to make this chap blind. After all, a man who looks like that could pick anyone he likes to go and do symbolic things with, but the trouble is, he wouldn't be able to see me from the terrace then, would he?) Anyway, he takes my hand as we pass between the tall hedges, and a jolt of electricity seems to shoot through my body. Suddenly the rules I have tried to live by mean nothing, because on this day, at this time, in this place, I know that there can be no other law but the law of passion.

We reach the centre of the maze and he turns to me, his smouldering eyes ablaze with passion (actually, I suppose if they're smouldering, they can't really be ablaze as well, can they? Still, never mind – you know what I mean) and my whole being is filled with urgent awareness that the *moment* has come.

The fantasy does tend to break down a little at this point. One option is that we make wild, passionate love there in the centre of the maze, but the practi-

calities make this a little tricky. How quickly, for
instance, would I be able to remove my matronly
figure from the full-length old-fashioned dress that I
had forced it into earlier (I never have been able to
fantasise a better figure for myself convincingly), and
if I did manage to get it off, what then? Assuming
that he wasn't put off by my matronly figure or the
time it took to unwrap it, where would the passion
take place? Seats at the centre of mazes are notori-
ously short and hard – made of wrought-iron usually,
I seem to recall. I certainly wouldn't fancy that. The
grass would be softer, I suppose, but you can't have
glitteringly dew-bedecked lawns at one point in your
fantasy and expect them conveniently to dry up a few
minutes later just because it suits you. I do like to be
consistent in these matters. Nor is it likely that
Smouldering Eyes would have brought something to
lie on – you just don't carry a spare tarpaulin under
your arm in stylish fantasies like mine.

The other option, and to be honest, this is the only
one which I find in any way satisfying, is that he and
I sit quietly down on one of the seats to talk about the
lives to which we must soon return. He senses in me
a sympathy and beauty of spirit that makes him long
to be with me always (matronly figure notwithstanding), and I yearn to reach towards the helpless child
that until now has cried out in vain from within his
manly exterior, but we both know that it can never
be. At last he stands to leave. We part bravely. There
is one, sweet, never-to-be-forgotten kiss, and then he
is gone, turning his face away quickly so that I shall
not see the tears that already blur his vision.

I sit motionless for a few minutes, mourning the fact that something so fragile and so fleeting has disappeared for ever from my life. He has gone, and I am left alone at the centre, suddenly wondering how on earth I'm going to find my way out of this blinking maze.

I chuckled out loud at this point in my reflections, causing the Robinsons' neighbour, Mrs Van Geeting, to glance up from the flowerbed that she was prodding with a neat little garden fork. Mrs Van Geeting was a long-widowed, white-haired, but very sharp old lady in her late seventies, who, despite her alleged addiction to a large daily intake of white rum, was amazingly fit for her age. I had met her several times since she moved in a couple of years ago, to be a few roads away from her son and his family, and we got on well, especially as I had been able to help sort out a little misunderstanding between her and Mike when she first arrived. She got on well with the Robinsons too, seeming quite entertained by the roller-coaster style of their family life. The ghost of a smile appeared on her face as she looked at me now.

'You know, Miss Reynolds,' she said, 'people who stand in the middle of the lawn laughing at nothing at all with scissors in their hands tend to get taken away eventually.'

I looked down at my hands and laughed again. 'Do you know, I'd completely forgotten what I came out here for. I was just on my way to get some brambles for the stick-insects, but the sun was so nice, and I got thinking about – this and that. I was in another place, miles away.'

Her eyes twinkled. 'Well, from the way you laughed just now, I wouldn't mind going on holiday there, wherever it was. Looking after the house, are you?'

I waved my scissors vaguely. 'Yes, sort of. Keeping an eye on things, you know.'

'I've always thought you might end up moving in with them', said the old lady in her forthright manner. 'You'd do them good. They think the world of you, you know.'

Embarrassed, I made a feeble protesting sound, and was about to say something else when the ringing of the telephone sounded clearly through the open kitchen door.

'You'd better answer that,' said Mrs Van Geeting, 'they might have got the wrong airline or the wrong day or the wrong planet or something.'

The slim, track-suited figure bent to her gardening again as I turned and hurried in to take the call. Shutting the kitchen door behind me I lifted the receiver from its wall-mounting.

'Hello – Dip Reynolds here, can I help you?'

'Oh, yes, err, hello, Dip, it's Daniel Wigley here. I just wanted to check with you and the family about tonight. Do you like steak, and is Mike there?'

Chapter Five

Because of Mrs Van Geeting's final words I was strongly anticipating that it would be the Robinsons who were phoning, so it took me a while to focus on the fact that the man's voice on the other end of the line was not Mike's. It was in fact a slightly odd man called Daniel Wigley, who attended our sister church, St Paul's, a man whom Jack said should have been shot long ago for not having already changed his name in case he ever got married and produced children who would have to endure the horrors of school life as little Wigleys. He was one of those square-shaped friendless men who need to shave twice a day but don't. He had recently confided in Mike, Kathy and me that he felt unjustly treated by certain members of his church, and was secretly convinced that no one really cared for him. For Daniel, taking offence seemed to be practically a hobby, and this, God help me, was the man who now wanted to check with Mike and me about something involving all of us that was supposed to happen tonight while Mike and the others were in an aeroplane over the Atlantic. Why had he asked me if I liked steak?

'Mike's not here just now, Daniel. The whole family is – out at the moment. Can I help at all?'

Daniel's deep, slightly fussy voice sounded again.

'Well, I simply wanted to make sure that I hadn't made a silly assumption.'

'Yes, what – ?'

'I felt that, as this is such a very important occasion, I should be a little more expansive than usual, and so I've decided that we'll be having rump-steak for our main course. I've been marinading all the steaks for the last twenty-four hours, but it occurred to me just now that some members of Mike's family, or yourself, of course, might not enjoy steak, or perhaps even be vegetarian, in which case – '

'Rump-steak!' My voice was filled with delight, my mind with unspeakable horror. I had interrupted in a desperate attempt to establish the actual dimensions of the impending disaster. 'My goodness, that *is* pushing the boat out. Tell me – I can't quite work it out – how many steaks is that altogether?'

'Oh, well, let me see, there's myself, five members of the Robinson family, and yourself, of course, so that's seven in all. I've also made a choice of three puddings, one of which', he laughed rustily, 'is my own favourite – marmalade tart, and there's a box of red wine,' another rusty laugh, 'so I think we need have no fear of being understocked in that department.' He paused. 'You think steak will be all right with everybody?'

'Oh, yes,' I responded enthusiastically, my mind racing, 'especially on an occasion like this. How, err, how would you actually describe the occasion, Daniel?'

'Well, I think', he replied, sounding a little surprised, 'I would simply describe it as a fiftieth birthday party, wouldn't you?'

Thank you, God!

I cackled hysterically, as though he'd said something terribly witty. 'I know *that*, I meant . . . '

Yes, what did you mean?

'I meant – how would you describe what this special day means to you personally?'

'Ah, yes, sorry, I see what you mean – well, of course, it is a significant milestone in my life, a happy life generally, although, as I think you know, I've felt let down from time to time by folks one should perhaps be able to trust. Our curate's wife has done her best to reassure me, but . . . Anyway, none of that matters today, because today is a time to celebrate with good friends, and I look forward to seeing you all at seven-thirty.'

Here was my last chance to blurt out the truth – and I couldn't. I wanted to, but I just couldn't do it.

'See you at seven-thirty', I trilled brightly. 'Byee!'

As I slowly replaced the receiver on its hook and leaned my forehead against the coolness of the kitchen wall, I was filled with a strange sense of calm. The situation I had been placed in was so appallingly, mind-blowingly awful, that its very awfulness had a kind of sedating effect. I sat like a statue on the nearest chair and reviewed the situation.

'Seven steaks sizzling.' I giggled hysterically suddenly as if I was tipsy. 'Three puddings doing something beginning with P. A world of wine wasted. Oh, dear, what am I going to do?'

Isn't it amazing how inventive the human brain can be when it comes to covering tracks or saving face? My own experience is that a sort of creative adrenalin begins pumping ideas up at a furious rate, much more so than when the same sort of mental energy is required for the benefit of someone else. It was true that in this particular case the fault was not really mine – it was Mike who had made this arrangement and not only forgotten it himself but forgotten to tell everybody else who was concerned as well – but I was, at the very least, almost a Robinson, and from the moment I had failed to be honest with Daniel I was as implicated as anyone else.

The first idea that occurred to me was the obvious one of illness. I could say that two or three of the family had been struck down by Ukrainian 'flu or something, and I and the others had to stay at home and look after them. Entirely adequate as an excuse, but, as a moment's reflection showed, useless in fact, because if Daniel met any friend of the Robinsons over the next few days and enquired about their health, he was likely to learn, not only that they were not ill, but that they were on holiday in America, and had been since the day when we were all supposed to go to dinner. No, it needed something much more radical than simple illness.

Suddenly remembering that I still hadn't collected lunch for Rowan and Kimberley, I picked up my scissors and wandered back out into the garden, pondering as I went. Another idea. What if I rang Daniel and told him that a phone-call had come just after he and I had spoken, to say that the Robinson's flight to America, which was originally scheduled for tomorrow, had been unexpectedly moved forward to today because of an error by the airline? Mike and the others were devastated, I could say, about missing Daniel's birthday celebrations, but they had just had to get everything together in a tearing hurry and go. Of course, I'd add, I would still love to come to dinner this evening if that was all right.

I nodded with satisfaction. That should work very well – as long as I grabbed Mike as soon as they got back and made sure he knew about the 'rescheduled' flight before he ran into Daniel. Yes, that solution would cover just about all the angles. Confusion over flights was an area that could be fudged to a point of total confusion, and the real beauty of this particular idea was that, apart from some anonymous (and imaginary) official buried deep in the bowels of airline administration, it was nobody's fault. I felt a touch of the wobblies at the thought of the actual phone-call to Daniel, but once that was done all would be well, and I might even get out of going myself.

I felt quite pleased and proud. An impossible problem solved by a little thought and ingenuity. As I bent to snip off a length of bramble that would undoubtedly be the equivalent of a large steak and chips followed by apple pie and custard, as seen through Rowan and Kimberley's eyes, yet another idea suggested itself to my fertile brain. I was drunk on my own cleverness. What about if I contacted some people from Daniel's church, threw myself on their mercy, and implored them to arrange a surprise party to which Daniel would be lured later in the day, before the hour at which the ill-fated birthday celebration was due to begin? At the moment when

Daniel, like some *This is Your Life* victim, learned with delight that he was, after all, cared for by his church community, I would make sure I was close to the Robinsons' phone, ready to graciously insist that neither the Robinsons nor I would mind in the least if the steaks went into the freezer and our dinner engagement was postponed to a later date.

A good plan, I thought to myself, as I crossed the lawn towards the house, trailing my bramble behind me, but there wasn't enough time left really, and – I stopped as a fatal flaw suggested itself to me. Aloud, I said, 'Why didn't they ask the Robinsons?'

'I've always wanted to be in an Agatha Christie book', said a voice drily from the other side of the fence.

I'd forgotten about Mrs Van Geeting, who was still working at her flowerbed a few feet away from me. The Robinsons' equivalent strip of cultivated ground was way overdue for weeding and thinning out, the narrow bed crammed with coarsely foliaged, yobbish weeds and plants, fighting and pushing and shoving as they battled for every cubic inch of soil and air. By contrast, the Van Geeting garden was inhabited by beautifully shaped, well-behaved plants who kept a suitable distance from each other and displayed their attractions in a proud but quietly civilized sort of way. Mrs Van Geeting was dropping a little handful of what looked like purple crystals into each weed-free space between her plants – some kind of nutrient, I supposed.

'I'm sorry,' I said, 'I was thinking aloud. I'm not even sure what I said.'

She chuckled. 'If you get murdered when you go back indoors and no one knows who did it, I shall have to tell the police that the last thing I heard you say, standing in the middle of the lawn with scissors and bramble leaves in your hand, was, "Why didn't they ask the Robinsons?" I just thought it sounded like something Monsieur Poirot might have tackled with those little green cells of his.'

I frowned. 'Grey cells, you mean, don't you? Wasn't it his eyes that glowed green when he suddenly knew who'd done it?'

'Whatever,' replied Mrs Van Geeting unconcernedly, 'colourful sort of chap, wasn't he? Fancy a cup of tea in the garden?'

Blessed postponement!

'Yes please, but it'll have to be a quick one. I've got a rather tricky phone-call to make in a moment. I'll tell you all about it. Give me a second to serve Rowan and Kimberley with their steak and chips and I'll be right with you.'

I enjoyed sitting in the next-door garden describing my problem and its possible solutions as I drank Earl Grey tea from a proper cup in a proper saucer. Mrs Van Geeting and I had enjoyed a very comfortable, occasional relationship since the day when I had saved Mike from the awe-inspiring wrath of his recently installed neighbour by managing to interpret one of his unfortunate attempts at making a joke. Actually, Mike's attempts to make jokes were never anything but unfortunate in the sense that they were never even remotely humorous, but like many people who joke very rarely, he sometimes fancied

88

he'd hit upon a retort or comment so side-splittingly hilarious that other people were bound to roll around in hysterics when they heard it.

On this occasion, responding to a gentle tap at the front door, Mike had discovered a nervous-looking small boy perched on the front step. The child, who subsequently proved to be Mrs Van Geeting's grandson, Luke, bravely delivered this tremulous speech:

'Please may I get my boomerang back from your garden, please?'

It was at this point that Mike saw an opportunity to exercise his flashing wit. How a man with his long experience of working with small children could have been so lacking in good judgement is impossible to say. Just about everybody else in the universe could have told Mike that making obscure jokes to nervous four-year-old children whom you've never met before is unwise, to say the least. I was sitting in the lounge next to the front door at the time, balanced on the edge of my chair in not-very-well-known-guest-on-her-best-behaviour-mode, so I heard every word of the dialogue between Mike and Luke. As far as I can remember it went as follows:

Luke : Please may I get my boomerang back from your garden, please?

Mike : (HERE COMES THE JOKE, IN CASE IT'S NOT IMMEDIATELY OBVIOUS) What I'd like to know is what you were doing in my garden in the first place.

Luke : (WITH LOWER-LIP TREMOR) I didn't come in your garden. I only been in Gran's garden.

Mike : (REALIZING THAT, INCREDIBLY, THIS CHILD HAS NOT UNDERSTOOD HIS BRILLIANT JOKE) Yes, I know, I meant that because it was a boomerang you wanted to get, you must have been in my garden in order to –

Luke : (BEGINNING TO CRY BUT PHYSICALLY PARALYSED BY FEAR OF BIG BULLYING MAN) I n-n-n-never went in your g-g-g-garden. I only been in G-G-G-Gran's garden.

Mike : (PANICKING SLIGHTLY) I know you haven't been in my garden – I didn't mean you'd really been in my garden. What I meant was that boomerangs are supposed to come back when you throw them so you must have been in my garden to –

At this point Luke burst into floods of tears and Mrs Van Geeting appeared on the scene demanding that Mr Robinson provide an explanation for the little boy's obvious distress. So overwhelming was the force of the elderly lady's grandmotherly defence of her charge that Mike became less and less convincing in his attempts to explain what had happened. Yes, he admitted, he had said that the boy had been in his garden, but he hadn't meant it. It had been a joke. Mrs Van Geeting begged to know what was even slightly funny about accusing a child of something he hadn't done and making the child cry. Mike said that the joke hadn't been that the boy had been in the garden when he actually hadn't, but it was to do with the fact that it was a boomerang he wanted back and not something like a ball. When Mrs Van Geeting replied to this statement she still sounded very cross, but an element of wariness had crept into her voice, and I decided to intervene before men in white coats were summoned to take Mike away to a place with nice soft walls where he could rave about jokes and balls and boomerangs to his heart's content. After I had joined the little group on the doorstep and quietly explained Mike's pathetic joke, all was well. In the end Mrs Van Geeting was highly amused, and as soon as little Luke finally understood that the big man was not a nasty man but a nice man who made silly jokes, his tears gave way to that watery rainbow chuckling which seems to be a common feature in very small people who are mightily relieved. He fetched his boomerang from the garden and we all had a drink together. From that day onwards Luke referred to Mike as 'The nice man who makes silly jokes', a title which greatly amused the rest of the Robinson family.

'So you're planning to tell this Wigley fellow a thumping great lie, are you?'

I was a little taken aback by Mrs Van Geeting's summary of my intentions. I hadn't really thought of it in terms of lying exactly, more as a kind of protection for Mike – and for Daniel, of course.

'Well, he'd be terribly hurt if I told him what's really happened, wouldn't he? He's already convinced that nobody cares about him – this would just about be the last straw for the poor chap.'

The old lady sipped tea and said nothing. Over the top of her cup the shrewd eyes, surrounded by hundreds of tiny wrinkles, held mine. I babbled on as though I was answering some fresh argument.

'It's all very well saying that people ought to be told the truth, but when it's hurtful I can't see the point. Mind you, I don't actually know what Mike would want me to do, and I suppose it's his problem in the end. He might want to be quite open about the fact that he's forgotten the dinner, and I don't want to put him in a position where he has to . . .'

My voice trailed away as I lost my grip on something that had seemed quite straightforward. This uncompromising person was absolutely right. I was planning to tell Daniel a thumping great lie.

'Tell me something.' Mrs Van Geeting placed her cup down on its saucer and leaned back in her chair. 'Why do you think Mike forgot about this Wigley man's dinner? I mean – what was the *real* reason?'

Dismissing immediate responses, I tried to make my mind into a still pond. It was a few moments before the truth bobbed up to the surface.

'Because he doesn't really care about him.'

'Why doesn't he really care about him?'

'Because he's a tense, not very attractive person who's always complaining about the way other people treat him.'

'Does anyone ever tell him that?'

I thought about the people I knew at St Paul's and in my own church. No, we didn't do confrontational things like that. We kept the peace. We were Christians – or cowards, or both.

'I shouldn't think so, no.'

'Perhaps someone should. I don't follow your bloke, but I should think that's what he'd have done. I don't know how he would have put it, but I bet he wouldn't have told Wigley a thumping great lie.'

I thanked Mrs Van Geeting for the tea and the chat, and I meant it. I really was grateful, but I went back to the house feeling very chastened. It had taken someone who didn't follow my 'bloke' to show me where I was going wrong. I picked up my car keys, hunted out the Robinsons' disreputable address book in order to check where Daniel lived, took a few deep breaths to calm myself, and was about to leave when someone rang the front door bell. I nearly crept out through the back to avoid whoever it was. I'm glad I didn't, because when I opened the door, there on the step, looking very excited and very embarrassed, stood Daniel Wigley.

The shock of seeing Daniel really did take my breath away. People use that expression in books and it doesn't always sound very convincing, but that's exactly what happened to me. For a moment I thought I was going to faint. Fortunately, Daniel had so much to say himself that it didn't really matter.

'Oh, Dip,' he said, his eyes full of the strangest mixture of anguish and ecstasy, 'are the others here? Mike and the others, I mean? Are they in?'

All I could do was shake my head dumbly. My lungs still felt like two stale kippers.

'Dip, I have to ask you all the most enormous favour, and I feel dreadful – awful about it, but, you see . . . ' He gestured towards a large expensive car parked in front of the house. I could make out the vague shapes of two people, probably a man and a woman, one in the driving seat and one in the back, peering in our direction. 'My brother and his wife – my only family – such a surprise to see them. Come to take me out for my birthday.' He waggled his hands with the passion of apology and joyful anticipation. 'Please – *please* would you forgive me if we were to arrange a different date for our evening together, only, you see . . . '

Daniel was one big knot. My breath had returned, so I untied him.

'Daniel,' I said (no dishonesty required here at all), 'I know without a shadow of a doubt that Mike and Kathy and the boys would want me to say that you must forget all about the evening we'd arranged and go and have a good time with your family. We'll get together some other time – don't worry. Just go.'

Throwing profuse thanks, humble apologies and promises for the future over his shoulder, Daniel went. He was relief personified. A final wave from the front passenger seat as his brother's posh car purred away up the hill, and he was gone. I stood in the doorway for a little while shaking my head. I felt perfectly calm but profoundly bewildered.

'You know,' I said very quietly to God, 'I'm beginning to learn never to trust you.'

I glanced up at the front wall of the house as a light breeze set the leaves of the Virginia Creeper rustling. The noise they made sounded like a round of applause on the radio with the volume turned down, or perhaps a little like someone laughing a long way away.

Chapter Six

The business of Daniel's birthday and that brief conversation with Mrs Van Geeting helped to clear my mind about what to say to the Robinsons when they came home. I decided that I would simply tell the truth, and, in the end, that's exactly what I did.

The family arrived back three weeks after they'd left, in a state of jet-lagged weariness, but, as far as I could tell, they had enjoyed their epic holiday. It was the variety of separate comments that fascinated and amused me more than anything when I went round on Sunday, the day after they returned. Mike, for instance, said that it had been 'absolutely marvellous from beginning to end!', while Kathy's summary was 'Mostly good with one or two hell-on-earth family rows thrown in'.

Jack silently (and discreetly) showed me a photograph of a very attractive young lady leaning against an airport luggage trolley and looking slightly weepy. To him I said, 'What a *lovely* girl.' To myself I said, 'What Large Phone Bills'.

When I asked Mark what he thought of America he said that he'd enjoyed going to see a real baseball match, and the food – particularly the beefburgers – had been 'well excellent', but apart from that, it was just like England really, and he didn't think he'd bother going again.

Felicity – oh, how I enjoyed seeing Felicity again –

was, of course, enthusiastic about everything she'd seen and done, but especially about something she said she'd brought back to make up for me not going to America. After annoying her mother with five minutes of insistent rummaging through the Robinsons' typically depressing rubble of half-unpacked luggage (nobody seemed to have any philosophy at all about *un*packing) she finally produced a nice little decorated box about an inch and a half square, and placed it into my hand with quivering excitement.

'I bought the box for you when we got off the plane back in England yesterday, Dip,' she said, bouncing impatiently on her toes, 'but that's not the really important thing. The really important thing's inside. Open it! Go on!'

I admired the prettiness of the box for a short time and then carefully prised the lid off. Inside was a very ordinary, irregularly shaped piece of grey stone. I took it out and held it between thumb and forefinger, trying to look as fascinated as Felicity obviously thought I was bound to be.

'It's a bit of America, Dip,' breathed my small friend, 'I brought you back a bit of America!'

Kathy, who was watching, smiled. 'Well, all I can say is – thank goodness that stone is in your hand at last. All we've heard for a fortnight is how pleased Dip's going to be when she gets her bit of America. We've lost it two or three times, and it was no use saying any other piece of stone would do. That's the one she found for you, and that's the one you had to have, and now you've got it.'

All the Robinsons brought back gifts for me, some of them quite expensive, and I genuinely appreciated every one of them, but there was something very special about that small coloured box containing such concrete evidence of love. I put it on my mantelpiece, so that every time a curious visitor looked inside and seemed to be wondering what the value of such a commonplace fragment of stone could possibly be, but didn't like to ask, I could take enormous pleasure in saying, 'Oh, that's one of my favourite things. It's a bit of America.'

I had decided to wait until the following day before giving the family my decision about moving in to live with them, but before leaving I took Mike into a quiet corner to describe the amazing saga of Daniel Wigley. The effect on poor Mike of suddenly remembering the arrangement he'd made for Daniel's birthday party was quite alarming. He clapped a hand to his forehead and seemed to shrink physically before my eyes, rather like an over-inflated, man-shaped balloon that has suddenly had its bung pulled out. He recovered a little as I went on to describe my wonderful hypothetical solutions, the significant chat that I'd had with his neighbour, and the heart-stopping appearance of Daniel himself just as I'd steeled myself to the prospect of driving over to tell him the whole truth.

'It all seemed terribly neat at the time, Mike,' I concluded, 'like one of those Christian books that make you feel useless because there's a miracle on every page. But when I think about it, I actually let poor old Daniel go off with his family thinking that it was him who had to apologize, and that's not neat – that's awful.'

Mike said nothing for a while when I'd finished, then he hugged me and kissed me on the cheek – hardly garden, maze and mansion stuff, but more real and very nice.

'I'm so sorry you had to go through all that, Dip', he said dismally. 'I felt sorry for him, that's what it was. Worst of all it was me who actually suggested to Daniel that one or two of us could pop round on his birthday because he sounded so fed up, and he got very excited and said we must all come to dinner, you as well, and I said yes, thinking that we could just – just go, and make him feel a bit happier, and then – well, it went completely out of my head. So much for me and my efficiency. Thank goodness for the brother and his wife coming along to be the cavalry for you.' He nodded soberly. 'I'm afraid dear old Mrs V.G. is absolutely right. Deep down I guess I didn't care enough to remember. But I'm really glad you didn't tell him a – what did she call it?'

'A thumping great lie.'

'Yes, one of them. Don't worry, I'll put it right. I'll go round and see Daniel later in the week and tell him what really happened. I'll do my best to be dead straight with him. Not easy, but I will try.'

Before leaving that afternoon I arranged to go round on the Monday evening, and asked that everyone could be there together for not more than about twenty minutes so that I could tell them what I'd decided to do. I felt quite frightened.

Some memories stay like photographs in your mind for ever, don't they? I can still see the assembled Robinsons on that Monday evening – Mike and Kathy like two bookends on the sofa, with Jack, their first edition, squeezed between them, Mark sitting stiffly in the armchair by the bookcase, and Felicity lying on her tummy on the hearth-rug, elbows on the floor, her chin cupped in her hands, gazing with untroubled expectancy into my face as everyone waited for me to say something.

'Before the holiday,' I began, 'you did something very beautiful for me. I don't just mean the banner that some of you worked so hard on, although that was *such* a good idea, and I've looked at it ever so many times since then – I've got it in my wardrobe now, hanging up at the back so that I see at least a little bit of it every time I go to get some clothes to wear.'

'Or when you go to put away the ones you've been wearing', added Felicity helpfully.

'Or to put away clothes, that's quite right, Felicity. It gives me so much pleasure to see it there, because every picture and shape tells me that I'm important to you. Much more important, though, is the fact that you actually asked me to come and live right here, and be with you all the time. I've spent the last four weeks thinking about that, and I've decided that my answer is yes – but not yet.'

Pause.

'When, then?' from the armchair.

How strange, I thought, that it should be Mark who reacted so immediately, and whose face clouded more quickly than any of the others.

'I don't know,' I answered, 'but when the right time comes I will know, and I do hope you'll still want me then.' Time for the most difficult and most important piece of truth now. 'I'm rather nervous, you see, that if I came and lived here all the time, you might find I wasn't quite what you think I am. When you live on your own for a long time you forget all sorts of things. You forget what it feels like to have little arguments or even big rows with people without them really meaning anything at the end of the day. You forget how to get up in the morning and be grumpy and not feel you've got to hide it and look as if everything's okay. It's such a long time since I had any practice at being in a family – being part of a family. I'm worried that I wouldn't be very good at it. I've got so used to being the one who listens and tries to help and stays calm and gets leant on. And I'm not like that at all really. I take all my upset and crossness and worry home to my little house and stuff it into cupboards and drawers because it isn't any use to anyone.'

This produced a little giggle of laughter from Felicity, who, I feared, had probably not understood a word I'd said so far.

'Coo, I wouldn't like to open your drawers, Dip,' she said, 'and have all that crossness and stuff jumping out at me like a lion. Do you like The Beatles, Dip?'

Seeing a mild rebuke hanging on Mike's lips I hastened to answer Felicity's question.

'Well, yes, I think I'd just stopped being a teenager when they became famous in Australia, and my friends and I used to listen to them all the time. Why do you ask?'

'Well, when we were in school the other day we had a student called Miss Barfield teaching us, and Miss Jarman said we had to be good because Miss Barfield's teacher from her college was coming in to watch her teaching us and – '

'Felicity!' interrupted Kathy rather testily, 'I hope this story isn't going on for too long because Dip's trying – '

'And it was easy being good,' continued Felicity, ignoring her mother completely, 'because Miss Barfield played some music to us, and one of the things was The Beatles singing a song about a lady called – something to do with football . . . '

The rest of us exchanged mystified glances.

'Rugby!' cried Felicity, sitting up and pointing a finger to the ceiling in triumph, 'That was it – Eleanor Rugby!'

A shadow of troubled embarrassment appeared in the little girl's eyes as we all laughed involuntarily. She swivelled her head, looking from face to face, trying to locate the source of our amusement. Jack slid down onto the floor and sat behind his sister with his legs on either side of her.

'It's all right, Flitty,' he said, putting his cheek next to hers and wrapping his arms round her chest, 'we weren't really laughing at you – it's just that you got it a bit wrong. It's Eleanor Rigby, not Rugby. You almost got it right. It just sounded funny.'

'Oh . . . ' Felicity trilled in a relieved sort of way, her eyes at peace again. 'Eleanor Rigby – that's right. Anyway, after we'd listened to it on the thingy, Miss Barfield said she was going to read the words out to us and we were going to say what we thought they meant. And when we got to the bit about Eleanor – '

'Rigby', whispered Jack.

'When we got to the bit about Eleanor *Rigby* keeping her face in a jar by the door, Jeremy Philips wouldn't stop laughing and Miss Barfield got cross and red and had to send him to sit outside Mr Wooldridge's office in the end, and then she asked us what we thought it meant, and I said p'raps she was a clown and wore a mask. But Miss Barfield said she wasn't a clown, but it was a *sort* of mask. She said that Eleanor – '

'Rigby', supplied Jack kindly once more.

'She said that when Eleanor Rigby got home she started to be who she really was and she stopped being how other people liked her being, and took her sort of mask off and put it in a jar next to the door ready for when she had to go out again. Is it like that, Dip?'

Nobody spoke for what seemed quite a long time.

I said, 'Just call me Eleanor', and then, foolishly, started to cry.

It all ended very well really. I felt a bit of a soft lump because they all crowded round and comforted me at the same time – even Mark patted my shoulder rather awkwardly. Later, over one of those miraculously reinvigorating pots of tea, Mike and Kathy suggested that I should have a key to their house, come in and go out whenever I wanted, and spend as much or as little time as I liked with the family until, as Kathy put it, I felt free to be 'as ratty and moody as everyone else'. I extended the same invitation to all of them, but I realized, even as I said it, that I didn't actually want people – not even the Robinsons – to walk into the place that was specially my own without any warning at all. I still needed a moment to dip into old Eleanor's jar. That awareness, and the fact that I kept my mouth shut about it, made me feel a little bit guilty, but it also made me feel a great sense of relief that I hadn't been too hasty in accepting the family's invitation. One day I would – probably – but until then I was happy to accept the title bestowed upon me that day by Jack.

'From now on, Dip,' he said, just as I was leaving, 'you are entitled to put DHR after your name.'

'Which stands for . . . ?'

'Detached Honorary Robinson.'

Chapter Seven

'Shall I tell you one of the most depressing things about being a parent?' said Kathy one blowy morning a few weeks later, as we hung clothes out in the garden together.

I replied through a mouthful of pegs. 'Only if you tell me one of the nicest things about being a parent first.'

Kathy threw back her dark head and laughed into the newly washed blue of the sky. 'I see. Another stage in the "Encouraging Katherine To Be More Positive Campaign", is it? You're all so subtle – I don't think. I can just hear dear old Mike's voice. "The thing is, Dip, that Kath does tend to get a little big negative about things from time to time, so if you get the chance to – you know – steer her into counting her blessings a bit more, it would be jolly helpful." Is that more or less the way it went?'

Kathy's impression of Mike's occasional parsonical style of speaking was such an accurate caricature that I dropped a towel into the flowerbed and nearly swallowed my pegs trying to catch it.

'Come on,' I said firmly, when I'd gathered myself and everything else together again, 'I refuse to be deflected. I want to hear at least one nice thing before you indulge yourself by wallowing in the most depressing one.' I pointed. 'Sit down there for a minute while I peg these socks up, and tell me what you've enjoyed about being the mother of three lovely children.'

Kathy flopped obediently onto the delapidated wooden bench that constituted the Robinsons' 'Garden Furniture'. Leaning back against the trunk of the ancient apple tree that supported one end of our washing line, she closed her eyes and thought for a moment.

'Well, I made a good start – I enjoyed conceiving them.'

I pegged another three socks up.

Kathy raised a finger. 'Here's a good one! They've made me laugh as much as they've made me cry, and that's saying something.' She opened an eye and grimaced questioningly in my direction. 'That do?'

'Hmmm, sounds a bit backhanded to me, but I'll let you off. Go on, then – what is one of the most depressing things about being a parent?'

She linked her fingers behind her head, and closed both eyes again. 'On a day like this, when the wind's whipping those sheets blindly around, and everything's coloured like a Ladybird book, I get sort of excited. I almost begin to believe that I might have a present – a now – of my own. Just for a second or two I get these tantalizing little nibbles and tastes of memory about how it felt to be me without constant reference to a houseful of other people. Tell you what, Dip, most of the time I feel as if I'm living in my children's pasts. I've indefinitely postponed being myself in order to serve them. I'm out of the current of my own life, if you see what I mean. I'm not even getting wet. I might as well – '

'Cold drink, Mum?'

Jack's unexpected arrival in the garden with two tall glasses of iced orange juice and lemonade stemmed the flow temporarily. I sat down on the bench beside Kathy, who sipped ecstatically from the glass in her hand. For a few moments we watched Jack as he strolled amiably back towards the house, banging the drinks tray rhythmically against his leg as he went.

'What was I saying?'

I cleared my throat and peered up through the leafy branches, seeking inspiration. 'Err, let me see, I think you were saying something to the effect that you have indefinitely postponed being yourself in order to serve your children. That's right – then Jack brought you a drink and you stopped.'

Kathy extended her hand, palm upwards, in mock emphasis. 'Yes, well, doesn't that just prove my point? I'm not even allowed to feel sorry for myself without one of them deliberately doing something completely out of character and spoiling everything.' She threw me a rueful glance. 'You must think I'm a perfect idiot, Dip, rabbiting on like that. I wish I hadn't said anything now.'

'Carry on with what you were saying,' I murmured, 'get to the end of your furrow.'

She smiled. 'Thank you for that interestingly agricultural image, Dip. Not terribly appropriate for one as delicate and prettily feminine as me, but never mind. No, seriously, I know I tend to exaggerate a bit, but there was some truth in what I said. You'll think this sounds horribly selfish, but sometimes I get razor-blade close to resenting the fact that I mother around like crazy in my children's early lives, making it all happen for them, trying to give them the possibility of becoming reasonably all right, happyish adults, while being fully conscious that I might well fail anyway. If Mark ever becomes famous he'll write about me in the *Sunday Times* colour supplement.'

Kathy moved her cupped hand through the air in front of her face, as though a double page was spread before her eyes.

'"The beginning of my life as a genuine personality was inevitably postponed until the day when I finally escaped the cyclonic context of emotional chaos that my mother created. We were trapped by an impassable wall of flying debris. The safe space was very small and exclusively designated by her. It may have been survival, but it certainly was not nurture."

'See what I mean? Why should I change his nappies when he's going to write things like that about me?'

When I'd stopped laughing I said, 'Has it ever occurred to you, Kathy, that your children don't actually need a good mother, which is what you're frightened you'll never be, because all they really want is *you*?'

'Take this Thursday, for instance.' She hadn't heard me – this furrow was even longer than I'd thought. 'This Thursday I have to go down to Felicity's school at two-thirty for the Infant Sports afternoon. As far as my darling daughter is concerned there never has been, and never will be

(Olympic events included) a more important sporting occasion than the Girls Running Backwards Throwing A Beanbag Up And Catching It Again Race, in which contest she has immodestly high hopes of success because her nearest rival, Penny Martin, has – Praise the Lord! – twisted her ankle. I always feel horribly threatened when I'm surrounded by all those perfect mothers, but, as far as Felicity is concerned, it's absolutely vital that I'm there on Thursday, smiling and encouraging and all the rest of it. And yet, I don't suppose the child will have any recollection whatsoever of this particular sports day or my contribution to it when she's an old lady of twenty-one.'

Later that day I joined the family for supper (a meal that was indeed regularly punctuated by Felicity's excited references to the pleasure with which her mummy would witness her victory in the Girls Running Backwards Throwing A Beanbag Up And Catching It Again Race on Thursday) and sat with them afterwards in the lounge, where all of us except Mark, who had 'gone out', found ourselves watching one of those appallingly saccarine television shows in which people are publicly and tearfully reunited with long-lost loved ones. I have always claimed to loathe these emotionally voyeuristic programmes, but, as usual, I eventually became aware that a soppy grin had glued itself onto my face like a mask, entirely without permission, and that my eyes were swimming with tears. It was some consolation to discover that the same soppy grin was plastered over each of the Robinson faces as well. At least we were all mad together. I expect it was this treacly atmosphere that made Kathy's sudden explosive outburst seem all the more alarming when it came.

'Oh, no! Oh, blast! Oh, sh– '

Four sentimentally tear-bedewed pairs of eyes turned towards Kathy, whose hand was now placed flat over her mouth, as if to prevent the escape of further, perhaps even more forceful, exclamations. Felicity sat up straight on Mike's lap and took her thumb out of her mouth.

'What's the matter, Mummy?'

'Nothing, sweetheart,' replied Kathy indistinctly through her hand, her eyes bulging with some undisclosed horror. 'I – I thought I thought something, but then I realized I – I didn't think it, so it doesn't matter. It wasn't anything. It was nothing. Watch the programme. . . . '

Nodding with childlike credulity, Felicity reinserted the damp thumb, and curled into her daddy's lap again. Mike looked at his wife, his expression saying quite clearly – If I pursue this, am I going to wish I hadn't?'

'Anything wrong, Kath?' he enquired mildly.

Kathy stood up, her face ashen. 'Nothing you'll be able to handle, Michael.' In unnaturally calm tones she added, 'It's going to make you very cross indeed. Dip, would you mind very much stepping out into the kitchen with me? I'd appreciate your advice on a certain matter.'

As I followed Kathy into the hall, and closed the lounge door behind me, I heard Felicity say, without a trace of concern in her voice, 'Mummy's done something wrong, hasn't she, Daddy?', and I just caught Mike's contained but ominously grim reply, 'Yes, darling, and a little bit later I'm going to find out what it is.'

Kathy already had the sherry bottle out by the time I reached the kitchen. She poured the rich brown liquid into two small glasses and put one of them into my hand with an air of doom-laden finality.

'Would you care to have a drink with me before the battle?'

I pulled a chair out and sat down.

Kathy raised her glass in ceremonial fashion. 'Those who are about to die salute you. Cheers!'

'Cheers – Kathy, what on earth have you done? Whatever it is, it can't be that bad, surely?'

She lowered herself slowly onto the chair at the end of the table, placed her glass down with concentrated precision, and heaved a very deep sigh.

The details of Kathy's face are oddly elusive. Sometimes, especially when she is very happy, or passionately angry on someone else's behalf, her face is truly beautiful, full of life and fire. At other times her features seem to lose their distinctness, the flush goes from her cheekbones, and the skin on her face turns to a parchmenty colour. The fire was certainly out now. My friend looked like someone much older and much younger than she really was.

'It is that bad, Dip. I can't believe it. It's a nightmare. I've double-booked myself for Thursday afternoon. While I was sitting in there just now watching that stupid programme, crying because one person

I've never met was unexpectedly confronted with their second cousin twice removed who is another person I've never met, I suddenly realized that Felicity, whom I have met and claim to care about, is not going to have her mother there on Thursday to see her win the Girls Running Backwards Throwing A Beanbag Up And Catching It Again Race.' She took another sip of sherry and shook her head slowly from side to side. 'What am I going to do, Dip?'

Looking at Kathy's troubled face, I reflected on the fact that I never know what to say to people when they get into this sort of state. I have come to believe, however, that this 'not knowing' is a significant advance on thinking you know what to say. There was a time when I responded to other people's difficulties with a sort of bullying exasperation, probably because I secretly thought that no one could have problems as mountainous as mine. Why should I waste more energy than was absolutely necessary on the trivial little blips that interrupted their smooth-running lives? The tendency to react like that was still in me, but nowadays I tried to kick it out as soon as it appeared. I have to be honest and say that Kathy's earlier complaints about the pressures of motherhood had provoked a little *'What about me?'* cry in some back chamber of my heart, but stronger than that response was the gritty knowledge that real friendship means accepting the whole package, and not just the bits that appeal to you. Kathy was much brighter than me in many ways, but her capacity for standing in anyone's shoes but her own was very limited unless she was made to do it.

I remember, for instance, an occasion when I tried to communicate the loneliness of being single to her. 'You come home after a hard day at work,' I explained, 'and once you've shut the front door behind you, everything goes quiet and you're on your own. You hang your coat up, put the kettle on, go up and change into something comfortable, then come down and make yourself a cup of tea. After that you might plonk yourself down in front of the television or read a book, and, more often than not, that's it for the rest of the evening. You might cook something if you've got the energy, or not bother if you don't feel like it, and all that's left after that is bed – on your own.'

Kathy listened intently to every word of this sad description of solitary living, nodded solemnly for a moment, and said in almost reverential tones, 'It sounds absolutely *wonderful* – except for the sleeping on your own bit, and that would be all right most of the time. . . . '

I tried to be quietly practical. 'Is there no chance of doing something about whatever it is you've organized for Thursday?'

Kathy's laugh had a very hollow ring to it. 'Yes, I could cancel it altogether, Dip. Then Mike would be furious with me because I'm not at his mother's house to stop her antagonizing the social worker who's coming to talk about her new bathroom, after months and months of trying to fix it up. He's going to be furious with me anyway because I didn't check the dates when I made the appointment, and Felicity's going to be in tears because I wasn't there last year either, and Jack's going to do one of his chilled disapproval numbers, and – oh, we *are* going to have a jolly time. I think I'll go and hang around outside the video shop with Mark and his mates tonight. He'll be the only one speaking to me by then.'

'But surely Mike will understand that you didn't mean to make a mistake, won't he? What about Daniel Wigley?'

Kathy leaned back in her chair and folded her arms. 'Dip, I have a feeling that, as far as Mike is concerned, I have used up my spiritual quota of forgiveness when it comes to this kind of mistake. Seventy times seven, isn't it? Well, my total must be way over four hundred and ninety by now. Daniel Wigley brings Mike's score to about three. No, any moment now he's going to come through that door with some puny excuse for being here and he's going to ask me what I've done. When I tell him what I've done he'll go puce, then he'll breathe very deeply, ask me how I could possibly be so disorganized, release one extremely cross exclamation and suggest that we pray. Then I shall get cross with him and burst into tears. Then Felicity will come through to ask what's the matter. Then Mike will tell her that her mummy isn't going to see her win the Girls Running Backwards Throwing A Beanbag Up And Catching It Again Race after all, and she'll be heartbroken and weep loudly. Then Jack will appear to rescue his little sister from her wicked, warring parents and I shall probably get cross with *him* as well.'

'But if you know all that's going to happen, isn't it possible to – '

'Kath, I think Felicity ought to go up now, don't you?'

Mike hadn't quite come into the kitchen. He had leaned round the door and spoken with casual lightness – a brave attempt to convince himself and us that, after a quick word, he would be off again to put his daughter to bed. Kathy passed the tip of her tongue slowly over her top lip before speaking.

'The answer to your unspoken question, Mike, is as follows. I have managed to arrange an appointment about Mum's bathroom at last, and I've organized for me to be there to make sure the social worker doesn't get savaged. I'm sorry, I meant to tell you I'd fixed it.'

For a moment Mike's eyes lit up – so far the news was good. 'Well, that's great, Kath. What's wrong with that? Well done! It doesn't matter that you forgot to tell me. The important thing is that something's happening at last. Just let me get our young lady up and then we'll have a chat about it.'

'Unfortunately,' continued Kathy in a dull monotone, 'I've arranged the meeting for this Thursday afternoon, and that means that I can't go to Felicity's sports and nor can you because you've got the Calais trip, and anyway it's me she wants because I cocked it up last time and it's all she's talked about for weeks. That's about it really – oh, except that I wish I was dead.'

There was something almost comical about the way in which Mike's body became frozen into its leaning-round-the-door position as he accommodated this extra information. At last, he straightened up, came into the room, and, leaning back against the closed door, dug his hands deep into his pockets. Then, just as Kathy had predicted, he simply went a sort of maroon colour, and began to breathe heavily through his nose. Missing out the anticipated 'How can you possibly be so disorganized?' phase, he moved straight on to the 'one cross exclamation'.

'You make me so *angry* sometimes!'

As usual, Mike expressed his anger as though he'd accidentally taken a foreign body into his mouth with a forkful of food. It had to be spat out, but he would much rather it hadn't got in there in the first place.

Still breathing heavily, he turned away for a moment, his shoulders rising and falling as he wrestled for self-control. Spinning round he said, 'There's no point in getting angry and upset – I think we should pray.'

'What do you mean there's no *point* in getting upset?' Kathy somehow managed to sound guilty and scathing at the same time. 'I've done something stupid, haven't I? What's the point of diving into prayer like some frightened rabbit going down a hole just because you can't handle a bit of real emotion? Get angry, for goodness' sake – and I'll get upset and cry. Why is that such a problem? It's not a problem for me I can assure you! In any case, praying isn't going to get me to Felicity's sports. Poor little girl – she's going to be so *very* disappointed.' And then, as if to fulfil her own prophecy, she buried her head in her hands and burst into tears.

I doubt if Mike's anger has ever been able to survive someone else's tears. Visibly shaken by the whole business he sat down beside his wife and sighed in despair. 'I still think we ought to be able to pray', he said rather defeatedly. 'We are Christians, after all.' He looked at me. 'I'm sorry about this, Dip, we seem to lurch from one crisis to another. I don't know how we manage it.'

'You mean you don't know how *I* manage it', snuffled Kathy. 'I shovel together great piles of guilt like some sort of emotional navvy. Guilty about screwing up the arrangements, guilty about getting annoyed with you when I should have got annoyed with myself, guilty about not wanting to pray and guilty about going on and on about how guilty I feel when I should be thinking of Felicity instead of me.'

Mike reached behind Kathy and pulled off a sheet of kitchen roll. 'Here you are, Kath,' he said, putting an arm round her shoulders, 'mop yourself up, or we shall all be swimming.'

So nice.

Stop crying, Kathy Robinson, you've got a nice man.

'Say a prayer if you want to, Mike.' Kathy sniffed and sounded like a scrappy little girl. 'We've got to do something.'

'There's no need for you two to pray,' I announced, 'I've been praying since Kathy and I first left the lounge, and, what's more, my prayer has been answered, so everything's going to work out just fine.'

Silence. They stared at me as if I'd unguardedly revealed a trace of insanity. But it was true – I had been talking to God ever since that loud exclamation had interrupted the flow of treacle a few minutes ago. I was beginning to learn that it was better to get on with praying while my friends went through the dramatic patterns and processes that seemed to form a part of every minor and major crisis in their lives. It was a nice feeling, because God and I loved the Robinsons. I could almost see his smile shining in their direction, and I could feel in my own heart how warmly he received my prayers for them. If only I could feel as confident about praying for myself.

'Do you mean an answer about Felicity and the sports, Dip?'

'Yes, Mike, it's all sorted out.'

A small candle of hope began to burn in Kathy. 'What is the answer, Dip?'

'I suppose it sounds a bit conceited really, but, well . . . the answer to my prayer is me. *I'll* go to Felicity's sports day on Thursday.'

The candle flickered and went out. 'Oh, Dip, that's very sweet of you, but it isn't really an answer. I promised Felicity faithfully that I would make sure I was there to see her this year, and she's reminded me of it on and off for the last twelve months. I know she'd love you to come as well, but it's *me* who's got to be there.' She slapped her hands down on to the table in anguish. 'Oh, Mike, I can't bear to see her face cloud over when I tell her. I hate the way our children suss me, one by one. I'm sick of being the way they find out the world isn't as perfect as they thought. I've *got* to be at Mum's – I've just got to be, or it'll all go wrong. . . . '

Seeing that she was about to dissolve again I interrupted hurriedly. 'Kathy, I said my prayer was answered, and it is. I know Felicity needs you to go, but if you leave me to put her to bed tonight I'll guarantee that the problem will be solved.'

Kathy didn't look very convinced, but Mike patted her shoulder encouragingly. 'Leave it to Dip, Kath, she's a bit of a wonder-worker sometimes, isn't she? You carry on, Dip, you know where everything is. We'll stay down here and beam hope up through the ceiling or something.'

Isn't it awful when you've made some grandiose claim and then have to justify it? All the optimism drains out of your body and you wonder how easy it is to emigrate to Tibet. It wasn't, in this case, because I didn't mean what I'd said. I felt quite confident that God, or some portion of the common sense of God, had spoken to me and suggested a solution to Kathy's dilemma. It was just that the gap between saying and doing has always felt an immense one to me. Two very different kinds of courage are needed. I have enough trouble with the theory, let alone the practice.

Felicity was snuggled up cosily with Jack, contentedly watching something highly unsuitable, when I went back to the lounge. She waved the four fingers of her right hand at me without taking her thumb out of her mouth.

'Bedtime, Felicity,' I smiled.

The thumb came out. 'Who's taking me?'

'I am. D'you want a piggyback?'

Children of six are generally incapable of faking their responses, and children like Felicity even less so. Please don't think it terribly strange if I say that, as usual, the child in me sighed with pleasure when my little friend rushed across to me, whooping delightedly, at the news that I was putting her to bed.

'Stand by the stool, Dip! Ready? Can I have a duck story in the bath?'

'Yes, I should think so. Say goodnight to Jack.'

''Night, Jackie!'

'Don't call me Jackie – Goodnight, darlin'.'

'What about Mummy and Daddy?'

'They'll come and say goodnight in a minute.'

'What about Mark?'

'Out, sweetheart. Hold tight, here we go, up the mountain!'

Minutes later Felicity was sitting cross-legged in the bath surrounded by bubbles, dabbing at her face with a flannel while I searched for the plastic duck that had become an essential part of bathtime routine when I was in charge.

It wasn't easy to find things in the Robinsons' bathroom. For some reason no one was bothered about taking out anything that they'd brought in. It contained a bewildering array of clothes, magazines, bath-dampened books of various kinds, forests of redundant toothbrushes, clusters of half-used bottles of hair conditioner, several shampoo containers (usually empty), the odd watch that had been removed from a wrist and then forgotten, a box of Felicity's face-paints in which the colours swam together in pools of water, plastic toothpaste dispensers caked with stripey gunge around the nozzle, sad demoted drinks beakers full of Jack's disposable razors – used but not disposed of – and an extraordinary selection of towels, varying from highly disreputable to plump, soft and newly washed. Every now and then Mike would revolt and produce complex check-lists and rotas designed to 'solve' the bathroom problem, but as no one ever made any real effort to follow them and he always broke his own rules within twenty-four hours anyway, the situation never changed much.

I found the red duck at last in the bottom of a large blue china vase that had found a home under the sink since I last excavated the bathroom contents. I held it up triumphantly.

'Hurrah!' cried Felicity, clapping her soapy hands together so that feathery wisps of froth flew around her head. 'Time for Ducky story.' Felicity's language quite often regressed to three-year-old level at bed-time.

The story about the duck had started its life on the very first occasion when I supervised bath and bed, and had been in steady demand ever since. For Felicity it was certainly a comfortably familiar ritual (she insisted that every detail should be exactly the same each time), but it had come to mean something even more significant to me. For reasons that I could hardly face myself, let alone reveal to anyone else, the telling of this very simple tale had an almost sacramentally calming effect on the most troubled part of my spirit.

As usual I started by placing the duck on top of the bathroom door, which opened against the side of the bath. Felicity gazed up at it with a dreamy little smile of happy anticipation.

'Once upon a time,' I began, 'there was a very, very lonely little duck who lived right on top of a big hill. He was ever such a nice duck really, but he didn't think anyone else could ever like him. "I'd love to have a friend all of my own," he used to say, "but I don't suppose I ever shall. Who'd want to be friends with a silly red duck who's too frightened to come down from his hill and doesn't know anything about anything? No," he sighed, "I shall never have a real friend."

'Every day the red duck would climb to the very top of the hill' – here, I always walked the duck along the top of the door until it was directly above Felicity – 'and look over the edge of a very steep cliff. Far, far below, he could see a little girl bathing in a beautiful lake, and each time he saw her he wished so much that he could be down there as well, swimming around and making friends with the little girl, who' – an invariable addition, this – 'looked almost exactly like you, Felicity.'

I walked the duck to and fro along the top of the door, tilting him over the edge each time he got to the end.

'Every single day he trudged to the top of the slope, gazed down at the swimmer below, then waddled home feeling lonelier than ever.'

This was Felicity's cue to tilt her head to one side, turn the corners of her mouth down, and wrinkle her eyes in pantomimic sympathy with the hero of my story.

'Then, one day, when the little red duck had climbed the hill yet again, and was feeling lonelier than ever, he leaned so far over the edge of the cliff to look at the little girl that . . . ' (I paused so that Felicity could move slightly to one side) ' . . . he lost his balance and fell all the way down into the lake beside her. Imagine that!'

The dropped duck landed in the bath with a diminutive 'splish!' This was the bit that Felicity liked best. 'Hello, little duck,' she said, 'where have you come from?'

'The duck was terrified,' I continued, 'because he thought the little girl was going to be cross with him. "I'm very sorry," he said in a flustered voice, "please don't be angry with me for landing in your lake – I know you don't want to make friends with me because you've got lots of friends already, and I'll go away right now. Oh, *please* don't be cross . . ." But the little girl wasn't at all cross.'

Felicity plucked the duck from the water and gazed fondly into its eyes as I went on.

'"But, Duck, I haven't got any friends," said the little girl, "I'm a very lonely person. Every day I've seen you looking down from the top of the cliff and wished that I could be your friend, but I always thought you must have lots and lots of friends already. I was so pleased when you fell into the water beside me. Please stay and talk to me for a while." And do you know what happened after that?'

Felicity, who knew exactly what happened after that, shook her head, role-playing wide-eyed wonderment according to tradition.

'Well, they became really good friends – best friends, in fact, and they spent all their time together and they were very, very happy.'

'Good,' said Felicity contentedly, 'I'm glad. *I* wasn't very happy at school today', she added, lobbing her duck into the toothbrush forest, and adopting an expression of fierce gloom with such suddenness that I couldn't help laughing. 'It was awful. Can I get my hair wet?'

I picked up one of the plump towels from the rack by the wash basin and spread it out wide. 'No, you can't. Out you come now – are you going to do a jump?'

Felicity hoisted her dripping, skinny form up on to the side of the bath and, after balancing precariously for a moment, threw herself into my arms and the towel with such abandon that I nearly lost my balance.

'Can I go back down when I've got my nightie on?'

'No.'

'Daddy says it's all right as long as I remember to put my pants on.'

'That's only when you're allowed to go back down, and this time you're not, and if you argue I'm going to tickle you till you squeal.'

She dug her chin into her chest and grinned. 'I'm not going to argue, Dip. Dip, it *was* awful.'

'This thing that happened at school, you mean?'

'Yeah – awful!'

By now we had arrived in the bedroom. After being set down, Felicity let her towel drop to the floor and began to execute a naked, stomping war-dance on top of it. I tried to imagine what might constitute an 'awful' experience in this child's careless, clear-eyed world.

'I'm c-c-c-cold!' she gurgled as she danced and waved her arms in the air.

'Well, dry yourself then, you silly ha'p'orth! That's what the towel's for.'

Freeze, with hands spread out like little stars, grimace, giggle – 'Oh, yeah!' – frenetic towelling.

At last she was dry, inserted into her Garfield nightdress and snuggled up in bed. 'Now,' I said, 'what was this awful thing?'

'Oh, yes, it was – Dip!' She sat bolt upright, her face full of emergency. 'I haven't done my teeth!'

Back to the bathroom. Forage in the forest. 'No, not that one, that's my old one . . . No – yes, that's it, the pink one with the squiggly handle . . . Have I done it long enough . . . ? Have I done it long enough *now* . . . ? Mummy doesn't make me do it that long . . . I *must* have done it long enough now . . . Daddy makes me do it longer than that . . . Smell my teeth . . . '

Back in bed.

'Can I tell you about the awful thing now, Dip?'

'I wish you would. I'm getting quite worried about it. It's not a wild bear that hides in the teacher's cupboard and jumps out at children when they're sent to get something, is it?'

Felicity's eyes shone with delight. This was the

kind of game she loved. 'No, worse than that – *much* worse than that.'

'Worse than that, eh? Must be pretty bad, then – wait a minute, I know what it is!'

'What?'

'There's a wicked witch working in the school kitchen, and every day she puts a spell on one of the dinners, so that whoever gets that dinner turns into a bar of chocolate on legs until going home time. Today it was you, and you had to run around under the tables all afternoon to avoid being caught and unwrapped and eaten by the other children in your class. Or was it even worse than that?'

'Oh, *yes*, Dip.' Felicity, quite an accomplished thespian at the tender age of six, shuddered with horror. 'It was more frightening than anything that's ever happened to anyone in the world before. It really was!'

I scratched my head thoughtfully for a moment, then nodded slowly and solemnly. 'I think I know what it was. Your teacher took the class out to see how the fish were getting on in the school pond, but when you got there there wasn't a single one to be seen. And you were all standing quietly at the edge of the pond, leaning over to look and wondering where they'd gone, when a huge crocodile with big sharp teeth leapt out of the water and swallowed your teacher and your three best friends in one big gollup!'

'Not my friends,' edited Felicity firmly, 'three of the ones I don't like.'

'Ah, right, yes, of course, three of the ones you don't like – but still quite frightening, eh?'

'Yes, Dip, but nowhere near as awful as the awful thing that really happened. Go on guessing.'

She put her thumb in her mouth and smiled a crinkly, winning smile around it. Obviously this particular game could go on for ever as far as Felicity was concerned.

'All right, one more guess, only it's not really a guess because I'm pretty sure I've got it right this time. Let me see now – it was just coming up to playtime when a huge wind started to blow outside and the whole school was lifted up into the sky and blown far away across the sea to a cannibal island –'

'What's a cannibal island?'

'A place where people who eat each other live.'

'Oh, right.' Felicity nodded calmly.

'Yes, so, in the end, the school landed on this cannibal island, and when the headmaster and all the teachers and children came out of the front door –'

'We're not allowed to go out of the front door.'

'This was a special occasion, so you were allowed to this time. Anyway, when the headmaster and teachers and children came out of the door all the cannibals were waiting for you with spears and things, and there was a giant cooking pot full of hot water on a big crackling fire, and the cannibal chief said that as it was very nearly teatime somebody would have to climb into the pot to be cooked, and who would the headmaster choose? Would he choose a scraggy old teacher, or a nice plump little infant, or a stringy junior, and in the end – '

Felicity had replaced her thumb. Now she whisked it out again so that she could interrupt. 'In the end Penny Martin ran up and jumped in the pot without anyone telling her to because she can't bear not being first at anything.'

We laughed immoderately together.

'So, was I right? Was that the awful thing that happened to you? I bet it was.'

'Dip, it was *much* more awful than that.' She reached a wheedling hand out towards mine. 'Do some more guesses.'

I pushed the hand firmly under the duvet cover. 'No more guesses. It's your turn. If your awful thing wasn't a bear in the cupboard or a witch in the kitchen or a cannibal cooking pot – '

'You forgot the crocodile.'

' – or a giant crocodile, then what was it? And you'd better say it quietly so you don't scare me too much.'

Felicity propped herself up on one elbow and spoke in a dramatic whisper. 'This was it – I wore my new coat in the playground today, and it was too big. Whatever I did I was surrounded by bits of coat!'

'Oh, no!' I covered my face with my hands, over-come by the horror of this appalling revelation. 'When I was making all those guesses I never realized it was something as ghastly as that!' I parted my hands a little and peeped through the crack. 'Oh, Felicity, how you must have suffered.'

'Yes,' her voice wavered in true fairy-tale heroine fashion, 'it was awful. I kept wishing man-eating crocodiles would come along, or bears or something, to make me feel better, but they didn't.'

'Felicity?'

'Yes?'

'I wanted to ask you something.'

'What?' She was delighted with this new tack, unprecedentedly initiated by an adult at a point when sleep would normally be the next item on the agenda. I knelt down on the floor next to the bed so that I was nearer to her.

'The thing is,' I said rather haltingly, 'I've never had a little boy or girl of my own . . . '

Oh, Dances In Puddles, how you have longed for a little boy or girl of your own.

' . . . so I don't suppose I'll ever be able to do lots of things that mummies do with their children. That's why it's been so nice getting to know you and your brothers . . . '

'Because you can do some of them with us', said Felicity brightly.

'That's right, and it's been really good fun, but there is one thing I'd love to do that I've never done, and – well, I just wondered if you would mind.'

Felicity's mouth was agape with curiosity. ''Course I wouldn't. What is it?'

'You're going to think I'm ever so silly . . . '

'No I'm not.'

I looked down at my hands, spread flat on my knees. 'I've always wanted to go to a school sports day and be the special one who cheers for her little boy or girl and takes photographs of them as they run down the running track. I know you wouldn't mind me coming with Mummy on Thursday – '

'I'd *like* you to come', said Felicity earnestly.

'I know you would, darling. I was really wondering if, this once, it could be just me who came, so that I could pretend I was a parent and do all the things they do.'

'Like being in the Mummies' Running Race?'

'Err . . . yes, like being in the Mummies Running Race . . . ' I hoped the sudden draining of blood from my face hadn't been too visible.

'The thing is . . . ' Felicity's brows contracted as she thought through the problem. 'The thing is that Mummy really wants to be there this time because she was so upset about not being able to come last time, and she 'ticularly wants to see me win the Girls Running Backwards Throwing A Beanbag Up And Catching It Again Race.' She sucked air in through her teeth and shook her head rapidly from side to side with excitement. 'I think I might be going to win it, Dip, because Penny Martin's the only one better than me at running and catching, and she's – '

'Been cooked and eaten.'

Felicity's peal of laughter must have filled the house.

'Would it be all right,' I said, when she'd subsided a little, 'if just I came, or would that make you very unhappy?'

'I'll have to ask Mummy if she minds', replied Felicity with sudden gravity. 'Let's ask her now.'

I went to the door and called. Kathy came into the bedroom looking apprehensive and guilty. She bent over to kiss her daughter.

'Hello, sweetheart, have you had a lovely time? I heard you laughing . . . '

'Oh, that was about Penny Martin being cooked and eaten, Mummy. So funny! Mummy, Dip wants to come to my sports and take pictures of me and see me in the races.' The expression on Felicity's face as she continued was a remarkable approximation to the one I had seen Mike adopt when he was exhorting his children to be mature and reasonable about something that didn't appeal to them at all. 'Mummy, would you mind not coming this time, only Dip wants to be like a real parent, and' – a real clincher of an argument, this, as far as Felicity was concerned – 'she won't be able to be in the Mummies' Running Race if you're there as well, will she?'

'No,' said Kathy, with an even guiltier glance in my direction, 'no, I can see that, I really can. Well, as long as I can come next year I'm quite happy for Dip to take you this time, darling. Perhaps I'll go up and see Grandma instead, eh? That'll be fine.'

'You see, Dip,' Felicity yawned hugely, 'everything's all right. Isn't Mummy kind?'

'Yes,' I agreed, 'very generous indeed. Thank you, Kathy. Goodnight, Felicity.'

'Goodnight, Dip, thanks for my duck story. 'Night, Mummy.'

'Goodnight, my darling – sleep tight.'

When I looked in five minutes later the self-styled, odds-on favourite to win the Girls Running Backwards Throwing A Beanbag Up And Catching It Again Race was fast asleep.

Chapter Eight

On Wednesday evening I asked God to give Fletton Park County Primary School some sunny weather for their Infant Sports on the following day. Honesty compels me to admit that I also asked about the possibility of a freak storm that would last just long enough to wash away any chance of the Mummies' Running Race happening as planned. Mind you, if it had to be, then I was grimly determined that, for Felicity's sake, I would stagger through the event as best I could, but my heart sank every time I thought about it.

Thursday turned out to be a suitably sun-kissed day, blessed with one of those kindly breezes that prevent the heat from becoming unpleasant. I offered a trickle of thanks for this answer to prayer, and promised an absolute deluge of additional gratitude in the event of the freak storm being granted.

The weather was perfect, but the afternoon didn't begin very well as far as I was concerned, although I certainly took a huge step towards full qualification as an Honorary Robinson.

Arriving half an hour early, at one-fifteen, I made the awesomely dreadful mistake of parking in the staff car-park directly in front of the school.

'Well done!' I congratulated myself aloud on finding a place so easily, and had just dragged a comb through my hair preparatory to leaving the car, when a loud knock on the window made me jump. Turning my head I saw, on the other side of the glass, a very efficient looking female face ringed with very efficiently controlled grey hair. Also visible was a very efficient looking finger, prodding imperiously in the direction of the ground. I wound my window down. The voice that proceeded from the face was brisk and neutral in tone, but not actually unpleasant.

'Good afternoon, I'm Mrs Palmer, the school secretary – may I ask if you are a parent?'

My car is very small, and when you're sitting in it being talked to by someone whose face is very close to yours, and you think they might be about to tell you off about something, you tend to lose your head. The simplest and most trouble-free reply might have been 'Yes', because it would have come to the same thing in the end, but when I feel threatened I have a tendency to worship a tiresome and non-existent truth-monitoring deity who will 'get me' if I stray from the path of absolute, literal veracity.

'No,' I said, 'I'm not, but – '

'Are you here to see the headmaster, then? I'm afraid he won't be available this afternoon because the Infant Sports are due to begin in – ' she glanced at a very efficient looking watch – 'less than half an hour.'

She stopped speaking, but left her face where it had been. It was my turn to say something.

'No, I haven't come to see the headmaster. I'm here for the Infant Sports as well.'

I felt about four years old. The Face still didn't move.

'I'm sorry, I thought you said you were not a parent. Perhaps I misunderstood.'

Yes, you misunderstood! Yes, you in whose eyes I hardly exist at all, I am not a parent – but I have longed to be a parent. In my dreams I have lived a promise that no waking day has ever kept. I have known the pain of yearning for motherhood but never once the joy of holding my own flesh and blood. I am not a parent – yes, you misunderstood.

Some people, I reflected, and I'm one of them, become quite remarkably good at covering up the way they really feel. One of the greatest shocks of my young life was the news that a contemporary at college in Adelaide had narrowly avoided killing herself with an overdose of some kind, having left a note to say that social and academic pressure had become too much to bear. This girl and I had always got on very well, usually meeting at least once each day over a coffee in the college canteen. The thing that had always impressed me most about Grace was her laid-back approach to life. There was usually a lazy smile on her lips, and she had a witty, relaxed way of talking about things. She seemed to have such control over areas that created chaos in me. The last person likely to attempt suicide, I would have thought. When I visited Grace in hospital, at her request, the mask was off, and I was amazed by the contrast. I remember asking her why she'd never said anything to me about how she felt, but she just shook her head and said, 'Well, you don't, do you?'

And, of course, she was absolutely right. You don't, do you? At those times in our lives when we're really suffering, someone at work or at church or in the street will ask how we are and we'll smile and nod and say, 'Okay!' or 'Bearing up!', or 'Mustn't complain!', or 'Could be worse!', and all the time we're hurting like anything inside and we know they'll never really believe it if they find out later on, because our acting was too good. At one time I had the notion that people should be completely open with everyone about their troubles, but I don't think that any more. Nowadays I know that there's no point in telling everybody we meet how we feel when we're in agony. There aren't many folk, Christian or otherwise, who can wear someone else's pain. I think I could have managed a little of Grace's, though, and she did drop me a few of her pearls after that hospital visit.

The Face was waiting.

'I'm awfully sorry. I didn't make myself clear. I'm not actually a parent, but I've come to the sports instead of Felicity Robinson's mother, who can't make it this afternoon.'

'Oh, I see, yes – Felicity.' A slight lightening.

Surely the Face would go away now, and I'd be allowed to get out of my car and go somewhere where this person was not.

Please would you be kind enough to remove your face, so that when I open my car door I shall not have the sinful satisfaction of knocking you off your efficient feet? Lord, love her for me.

'Felicity Robinson, yes.' I smiled an end-of-conversation sort of smile and made little shifting movements to signal my intention of vacating the car. The Face didn't budge.

'I'm afraid it's not possible to park here, because the spaces are all reserved for teachers, but you'll find a large space behind the builders' yard next door. They've kindly agreed that parents should be allowed to leave their vehicles there on special occasions like this.'

A little imp sitting on my dashboard urged me to point out that I had already made it clear that I was not actually a parent, and to ask what parking provisions had been made for Friends Of Children on special occasions like this.

Shut up, Imp.

'I'm sorry, I didn't realize that. Over that way, is it?'

'That's right.'

'Thanks very much.'

'Felicity's a lovely child.'

'Yes.'

Nice Face.

I drove obediently to the right place and parked my car near the entrance.

I discovered the sports venue on the other side of what turned out to be a surprisingly substantial stack of school buildings. The newly-cut grass of the playing-field had been marked out with long straight white lines to create a running track for this very special occasion. Running down one side of this six-lane strip were three neatly arranged rows of the most disturbingly minute chairs I had ever seen, while on the other side two quite big children were placing rubber gym mats end to end, presumably to accommodate the mini-athletes when they arrived. Spaced out at measured intervals behind the mats were three poles on stands, each with a bell-shaped speaker attached to its highest point. Down at one end of the track a mixed group of adults and rather self-consciously important-looking older children were attaching pieces of coloured wool to what looked like little gold safety pins, and carefully laying a length of pink ribbon across the lanes, ready, I assumed, to be used as a finishing tape for the aspiring Linford Christies and Sally Gunnells who were soon to be going for Infant Gold.

I decided to sit as near to the aforesaid finishing line as I could get, a strategic point from which to observe closely the final stages of the all-important Girls Running Backwards Throwing A Beanbag Up And Catching It Again Race. A few parents (or friends of children, perhaps?) were already stationing themselves at this end of the track, looking rather oddly near to the ground as they lowered themselves on to, and in some cases totally enveloped, the miniscule blue chairs that had been provided for them. Gingerly, I took a seat myself, hoping that the thin tubular legs would not decide to sink slowly into the ground under my weight. Thankfully, they did not so decide, and quite suddenly, Mummies' Running Race notwithstanding, I felt a wave of happiness and well-being. The scent of cut grass was, as always, a poem of past times, and the sky was extravagantly, wastefully, wonderfully blue. I leaned my head back, closed my eyes and took in a long, deep breath of sun-soaked air.

Thank you, God, for unchangingly beautiful things.

I opened my eyes again to find that a collection of impossibly tiny children had left the school buildings and were moving in a happy straggle towards the running track. The straggle was headed by a most elegant, meticulously hair-styled lady in a flowing ankle-length dress. She held a small hand in each of hers and appeared to have several other little figures glued to her skirts by various parts of their bodies as she and they made their tranquil way across the shining grass. Arriving at the mat directly opposite the place where I was sitting, she sank slowly to the ground, drawing children with her as if, in filmic slow motion, they were filling a vacuum created by the descent of her body. The result was unconsciously artistic, as though the class had been posed for a Victorian photograph. If this is a teacher, I thought, then teachers have certainly changed since my early schooldays. I turned to the reassuringly untidy, friendly-looking person who was balanced on the Lilliputian chair beside me.

'Who's that teacher over there?' I asked, pointing across the track.

'Oh, that's Mrs Barcombe,' said my neighbour reverentially, 'she teaches one of the reception classes. She's really wonderful. Everyone hopes their children will start with her. Two of mine have and I'm hoping the last one will. They come home all warm and soft from her.' She smiled ruefully. 'I never seem to have that effect on them, so it's a good job somebody does. I'm Mrs Elphick, by the way. I haven't seen you before, have I? Have you got a little boy or girl here?'

I was much more relaxed now. 'No, I've come instead of a friend who couldn't make it. She's Felicity Robinson's mother.'

Instant recognition. 'Oh, I know Felicity. She's in class two with Claire, my middle one. Miss Jarman's class, that is. They go to Ballet and Modern together as well. Oh, yes, Felicity's been to tea. She was at ours with another friend called Emily the other day. She's a lovely little girl, isn't she? Marvellous imagination for games and that sort of thing.'

'Yes,' I replied, trying to sound like a detached assessor of loveliness and imagination, but actually feeling a deep sense of personal pride, 'yes, I'm very fond of her.'

'That's the other reception class,' said my new friend, pointing towards a second group of children issuing from the school buildings, 'Mrs Calne's class, that is. She's very nice in her own way. Her children learn all sorts of things, and I suppose that's what they're here for really, isn't it?'

Mrs Elphick's tone said, more clearly than words, that, in her view, the Calne method, which involved learning all sorts of things, compared very unfavourably with the Barcombe method, which sent newly-schooled children home to their parents 'all warm and soft'. Certainly, the flavour of Mrs Calne's regime was visibly different from that of the other reception class. She herself was a sensibly dressed, strong looking woman in her mid-forties with short-cropped dark hair and one of those square-jawed, scrubbed faces that I have always associated, probably wrongly, with vigorous female team-games. She marched at the head of a procession (not a straggle) of children who travelled in neat, hand-holding pairs towards the second mat from the end. Not for this class the graceful dying-flower descent of the previous one. After being arranged in a suitable pattern whilst still standing, the word of command was given, and they sat. Mrs Calne knelt tidily on one corner of the mat, and that was that. Turning her head, she flashed an unexpectedly sweet smile towards the beautiful Mrs Barcombe, who responded with a raise of the eyebrows and a friendly little shrug of the shoulders, as if to say, 'Here we go, then'.

Gazing across at the two groups of children, I was interested to note that the Calne children didn't really appear any less relaxed and happy than the Barcombe ones. They were just in a slightly different mode of behaviour, presumably because of the different types of control their teachers used.

Not for the first time I felt annoyed at life for failing to offer us nice, clear-cut heroes and villains. Why couldn't Mrs Barcombe be wholly wonderful, and Mrs Calne utterly horrible? A part of me had always wanted the world to be like that. Maybe there'd been too many story-books and not enough contact with flesh-and-blood people when I was little. People like me take years to get the real world into focus.

The rows of tiny chairs were filling up very quickly now as parents moved in a steady stream from car-park to playing field. Many wore sunglasses and carried cameras. Quite a lot had brought pre-school-aged children with them. There were babes-in-arms, wobbling glassy-eyed toddlers and sleeping tots in comfortable-looking buggies. All but the very youngest had been primed, no doubt, for that moment when an older brother or sister put in an appearance on the athletic stage. I hoped for the mothers' sakes that the sleeping ones would wake in time to enjoy the treat that had been promised to them.

The general atmosphere was one of buzzing expectancy, coupled with a rather odd air of corporate puzzlement. Because the rows of parents were stretched out over such a long distance from one end of the track to the other, it was difficult to imagine that one would ever really be able to discover what was going on until a race or event was actually under way. Most of the people around me wore encouraging, happy-to-be-here smiles in case their children happened to be looking, but while their mouths smiled their eyes peered blankly from side to side, hoping, I guessed, that someone would let them in on the secret of what had actually been planned. The three speakers on poles looked promising as far as this was concerned, but down below the finishing line a clump of worried heads bent over the microphone suggested that there could be problems in this area.

My neighbour, Mrs Elphick, told me that this was the first year they'd used a public address system (usually, someone called Mr Murray shouted) and she hoped they would get it to work, because in ten years of coming to sports days she couldn't recall ever having a clear idea of – as she put it – what had happened just now, what was happening at the moment, or what was going to happen in a minute.

Felicity's class was the last one to emerge from the school, and I must admit I felt quite nervous from the moment I spotted her relatively tall figure in the distance. Suppose she had forgotten it was I coming to her sports day instead of her mother? What if her face fell at that instant when she recognized me sitting among all the *real* parents? Like most of the other children, Felicity reached her appointed mat in a state of mingled excitement and worry. The reason for the excitement was obvious, but at first I hadn't quite understood the worry. My kindly neighbour explained.

'Most of them are checking that whoever's supposed to be here has turned up. You watch their faces when they suddenly see their special people – just watch.'

Felicity was no exception. I could see that total involvement with the thrill of the occasion had been temporarily postponed. Sitting cross-legged among her class-mates at the other end of the running-track, dressed in a white tee-shirt and little white shorts, hair neatly pigtailed, she scanned the spectators, her eyes moving from face to face with troubled concentration. I wanted to attract her attention, but all I could manage was a timid little wave of the fingers. When her eyes finally reached and met mine my heart stood still.

I needn't have worried. Seeing me flicked a switch

in Felicity. All the lights in her face came on, and she flapped her hands madly before settling down happily to chatter and giggle with her buddies.

Thank you.

'That's Mr Murray,' said my new friend, pointing to a figure that had just detached itself from the group of folk who had been worriedly examining the microphone, 'the one who usually shouts. The children really like him – he makes them laugh with his jokes. He's a good teacher too.' She giggled suddenly. 'Not what you'd call self-conscious about how he dresses, though, is he?'

It was a fair comment. Mr Murray, a tall, nicely built man, who might have been in his mid-thirties, was wearing what he obviously considered suitable garb for an outdoor sporting occasion. This outfit consisted of a pair of ludicrously long khaki shorts, two ancient black army boots surmounted by the merest glimpse of flimsy light-blue socks, and a violently orange, short-sleeved tee-shirt that just failed to meet the top of his shorts. The whole effect was topped off with a battered white floppy hat of the cricketing variety. Beneath the hat, Mr Murray's rather good-looking, pleasantly studious face was adorned by a pair of spectacles whose thick black rims seemed somehow to add an intensity of purpose to everything he did. Mrs Elphick was absolutely right. Mr Murray did not appear remotely self-conscious about his eccentric appearance, and, because he was so relaxed, he didn't really look funny at all. I have always rather envied people like that.

He strolled along the edge of the running-track past the long lines of parents, trailing the microphone lead behind him, his progress punctuated by little flurries of conversation and laughter as he paused to exchange a joke or greeting. He seemed to know nearly all the mothers, and even some of the little pre-school children.

'He looks like a nice man', I said mildly, as if I was commenting on a fairly agreeable piece of curtain fabric.

'Oh, he's *lovely*', replied my neighbour, her voice echoing the fourteen-year-old response that I had contained so carefully within myself. 'He can wear whatever he likes, as far as I'm concerned. Don't you think he's dishy?'

'Mmm, very nice.' I now sounded as though I might be talking about a *very* agreeable piece of curtain fabric. I had never described anyone (silently or out loud) as being 'dishy' in my life.

'Well, *I* think he's lovely,' said Mrs Elphick, her tone signalling a little disappointment at my lukewarm response. 'Oh, look, he's going to use the sound thing – the what-do-you-call-it? – the microphone.'

And indeed, the oddly dressed, dishy Mr Murray, now about two-thirds of the way up the track, having stopped and raised the microphone to his lips, was twitching his eyebrows and silently mouthing words as he prepared to speak to us all through the public address system.

'It'll be much better than other years', declared Mrs Elphick with comfortable optimism.

I have no doubt that it would have been better than other years – if it had worked properly. It wasn't that Mr Murray's words were not amplified, because they certainly were – three times in fact: once through each loudspeaker, at intervals of approximately half a second. The result was the sort of thunderously loud, cosmically-echoing, cloud-cracking voice that you'd expect to hear at the commencement of Armageddon, and all he had said was 'Good afternoon, everybody'.

A shocked silence fell, followed immediately by a ripple of laughter as the assembled parents realized they were not about to be judged by God, but addressed by Mr Murray.

'It was better when he shouted', commented Mrs Elphick.

Minutes passed as one or two practical looking staff members joined Mr Murray for prolonged and anxious discussion about various aspects of the sound system. Soon, we were being treated to further shatteringly dramatic attempts to impart information through the three speakers. The ranks of parents fixed their happy-to-be-here smiles yet more firmly on their faces lest their offspring should lose heart, and awaited further developments. Finally, from the loudspeakers came an unnaturally slow, sepulchral voice speaking in a low monotone, the sort of voice you would expect to hear if a major tragedy had to be announced from the stage of the Albert Hall.

'WE ... ARE ... HAVING ... A ... LITTLE ... TROUBLE ... WITH ... THE ... SOUND ... SYSTEM ... BUT ... IF ... I ...

SPEAK ... VERY ... VERY ... SLOWLY ...
AND ... CLEARLY ... YOU ... SHOULD ...
BE ... ABLE ... TO ... HEAR ... ME .... '

A round of applause from the parents, and a
chorus of near-hysterical laughter from the older
children on the mats greeted this extraordinary Vin-
cent Price impersonation.

'WE ... WELCOME ... YOU ... ALL ...
VERY ... WARMLY ...,' continued the voice in
terrifyingly ominous tones, 'AND ... OUR ...
FIRST ... EVENT ... WILL ... BE ... A ...
PRE-SCHOOL ... RUNNING ... RACE .... '

Six twitchily excited, but plainly bewildered, small
children were steered firmly to their places on the
starting line, and pointed in the right direction. Then
came the command, 'Ready, steady, go!'

This first event was not an unqualified success.
The six athletes concerned seemed to have absorbed
the fact that 'Go!' meant they were supposed to be
somewhere else, but only two of them had cottoned
on to the fact that everyone was supposed to end up
in the same place. The rest didn't so much run as
scatter in various unrelated directions. One plump
little girl dashed straight back into the arms of her
mother, who was seated near the start line, while the
little boy next to her turned around and ran as fast as
his legs would carry him in a direction diametrically
opposite to the finishing line. He stopped at the end
of the field by the hedge and started to practise roly-
polies in the long grass. Another decided to settle
down for a little sleep as nothing of great interest
seemed to be happening, and a fourth made her way

to the nearest speaker on a pole, where she stood gazing upwards in fascination as Mr Murray's doom-laden voice announced, 'I ... THINK ... WE ... SHALL ... HAVE ... TO ... BEGIN ... THAT ... EVENT ... AGAIN ....'

Expert child catchers were despatched to round up the six participants, including the two who had already finished the race. This pair returned looking a little puzzled, but they seemed quite happy to do it all over again. Soon, after some strenuous eye-level pointing and careful repetition of earlier instructions, the race was under way once more. This time, with the assistance of Mrs Calne, who, crouching low with her arms outspread, performed a sort of sheepdog role at the back, they all reached the finishing line to the accompaniment of wild parental applause.

Things seemed to go reasonably smoothly after that. Event followed event, each preceded by Mr Murray's sombre declarations. There really was something very strange about hearing the boys obstacle race, for instance, announced as though something sick and sadly dreadful was about to be perpetrated.

Many things made me laugh, but I had a secret cry as well. In the girls' egg and spoon race (introduced by Mr Murray as if we were being invited to witness a mass burial), five of the competitors finished more or less at the same time, but the sixth, a skinny little thing with thick spectacles, had been seriously delayed by her tendency to lunge wildly all over the track as she alternately lost and regained

147

control of her egg and spoon. It was as if some invisible, irresistible force took hold of the spoon every now and then and tried to drag it from her hand. The result was that she could only manage to travel in an average straight line. But she didn't give up. That was what brought the tears to my eyes. Long after the others had crossed the finishing line this heroine was putting as much effort in as she had done since the race started. When she did finally approach the end of the track her face was set in a mask of fierce determination. 'Who knows,' that face seemed to say, 'if I go on trying really hard right up to the end, even though the others have finished, I might still win! Who knows?'

I dried my eyes surreptitiously, and mourned the death of hope and innocence in all of us.

The moment for which Felicity had been waiting so long arrived at last. Like some Old Testament prophet foretelling the misery of Babylonian captivity, Mr Murray's voice echoed eerily across the field once more.

'OUR ... NEXT ... EVENT ... WILL ... BE ... THE ... GIRLS ... RUNNING ... BACKWARDS ... THROWING ... UP ... A ... BEANBAG ... AND ... CATCHING ... IT ... AGAIN ... RACE .... WOULD .... COM-PETITORS ... PLEASE ... TAKE ... THEIR ... PLACES ... ON ... THE ... STARTING ... LINE .... '

Felicity bared her teeth at me in a grin of intense excitement and gestured wildly towards the starting line. I nodded and waved enthusiastically to show that I'd understood. The great event was about to take place, but inside I suddenly felt sick. For some reason I had taken Felicity's chances of winning at her own valuation. She was unswervingly confident of success, but what if she was wrong? She could easily be wrong. Suddenly, the last thing I wanted was responsibility for dealing with a negative outcome to this race. I swallowed hard and waited.

The first part of the race seemed to bear out Felicity's self-assessment. By the time all the competitors had passed the halfway point, she was several yards in front and looking unbeatable. The difference between Felicity and the other girls was quite simple. Felicity could run backwards *and* throw a beanbag up and catch it. The others could only run backwards *or* throw a beanbag up and catch it. The result seemed inevitable, and the sensation of nausea in my stomach was just beginning to lift, when disaster struck.

As if he had been fired from a giant catapult, a toddler shot out onto the track and stopped abruptly, right in the path of Felicity, who, because of running backwards and concentrating on her beanbag, was completely unaware of the unscheduled obstacle. In a flurry of arms and legs, the two bodies collided heavily and fell to the grass in a heap. The toddler remained prostrate on the ground, roaring loudly for his mother, while Felicity sat up, rubbing her leg and looking dazed.

Even then, all might have been well. Grasping the situation quickly, Felicity jumped to her feet, beanbag still in hand, and having stepped round the small bawling figure, set off backwards once more in the direction of the finishing line. Unfortunately, she chose the wrong side of the toddler to continue her run, and immediately got tangled up with the child's mother who was intent on rescuing her son before he suffered more damage. By the time Felicity got going again and reached the tape she had been overtaken by all but one of the other runners. Instead of winning the Girls Running Backwards Throwing A Beanbag Up And Catching It Again Race, she had come fifth.

A great choking lump rose into my throat as I watched Felicity make her dismal way back to the other end of the track. Chin on chest, stiff-legged with containment of her grief, she was the embodiment of misery.

I shiver with horror when I think how close I came to making an absolute fool of myself and her. Everything in me wanted to get hold of whoever was in charge of this so-called Sports Day and insist that the race be run again so that a more just result could be achieved. Why, I would ask, should Felicity's dream be spoiled just because some silly toddler decided to run out on to the track? Perhaps, I would suggest, if the whole event had been a little better organized, with railings or something, it wouldn't have happened, and Felicity would be happy and smiling now instead of sitting on that mat over there, keeping her eyes tight shut to stop the tears from coming out. Thank God, I didn't do anything so awful. Instead, I found myself tidying my handbag with feverish intensity, as though the removal of chaos in one little world might help to unscramble the unfairness in another.

'Wasn't that a shame?' said Mrs Elphick with real compassion in her voice. I think she knew why I was tidying my handbag. 'You feel for them so much when it's like that, don't you?'

'Yes,' I said shortly, close to tears, 'you do.'

Even the dreaded Mummies' Running Race had lost its terrors now. As I panted down the track behind the lycra-clad figures of these very modern mothers a few minutes later, all I was conscious of was the glimpse I'd had of Felicity's eyes, large and shining with contained grief when I'd lined up for the start, and the crumpled little smile forced on to her face for my benefit just before the race began.

I came solidly last, of course, but apart from ending up in a state of near physical collapse, that didn't trouble me at all. The thing that troubled me was the prospect of driving home in the car with Felicity and coping with the weight of her unhappiness.

'THAT . . . CONCLUDES . . . THE . . . INFANT . . . SPORTS . . . AND . . . WE . . . WOULD . . . JUST . . . LIKE . . . TO . . . THANK . . . CHILDREN . . , STAFF . . . AND . . . PARENTS . . . FOR . . . HELPING . . . TO . . . MAKE . . . THIS . . . AFTERNOON . . . SUCH . . . AN . . . ENJOYABLE . . . OCCA- SION . . . . IT . . . WOULD . . . BE . . . VERY . . . HELPFUL . . . IF . . . EVERY . . . PARENT . . . COULD . . . TAKE . . . ONE . . . CHAIR . . . INTO . . . THE . . . SCHOOL . . . AS . . .

THEY ... LEAVE ... AND ... PLEASE ...
TAKE ... YOUR ... CHILDREN ... HOME ...
WITH ... YOU ... AFTER ... THEY ...
HAVE ... CHANGED .... THANK YOU ...
AGAIN .... '

Mr Murray's final message from the Pit Of Hades provoked a little patter of applause from the parents, and was followed by a general buzz and clatter of departure and clearing up. I thanked the friendly Mrs Elphick for her company, then picking up my miniature chair, walked slowly towards the school buildings. As Felicity's class passed me on the way back to their classroom I called out, 'See you in the car-park, darling – no hurry, take your time.' She flapped a sad hand and nodded in mute agreement.

Sitting and waiting in Daffodil a few minutes later I mentally rehearsed a variety of potentially comforting comments.

You did your best, that's all that really matters.

You'll have another chance next year, and you're so much better than the others that you're bound to win.

Your class did well in the team games, and you were involved in all of them.

It doesn't do you any good to get upset – try to think of something nice that's going to happen soon.

Cheer up! It's not the end of the world.

Pull yourself . . .

. . . *together. I really can't believe you're getting yourself in such a state over a stupid mouse, Elizabeth. Anyone would think you'd never had anything else that meant anything to you. We'll get you another one if it's that important to you. You've got a party coming up on Thursday – think about that instead. All right, well if you can't stop crying you'll just have to go and sit in your room until you can stop. . . . Getting angry and being rude won't help either, Elizabeth Reynolds. We don't want to see your temper – or hear it. Go on, off you go, up to your room! When you've learned to control your feelings you can come back down and be with us. No, I don't want to see you again until you can smile at me – and mean it. We seem to have been through this so many times. . . .*

The sound of the passenger door opening took me by surprise. My thoughts had been far away in space and time. Clutching her lunch box and reading folder in one hand, Felicity climbed in and clunked the door shut behind her. We looked each other in the eyes momentarily, a forlorn little girl and an anxiously perplexed middle-aged woman.

'I didn't win, Dip.'

'I know.'

'I came next to last.'

'Yes, I saw.'

Felicity's bottom lip started to tremble. 'I really, really thought I was going to win, Dip. I really thought I was.'

I don't want to see you again until you can smile at me. . . .

My bottom lip started to tremble as well. 'Darling Felicity, it must have been the most awful, awful feeling in the world, and I'm so sorry you didn't win. I bet you want to cry and cry.'

That was what she wanted. Dropping her lunch box and her reading folder on to the floor of the car, my small friend stretched her arms out to be held, and sobbed on my shoulder for at least a minute. I had a bit of a weep as well – mostly for Felicity, but partly for another little girl.

By the time we arrived home the tears had all gone, and Felicity was smiling at me again – and meaning it.

'Did you feel like a real parent today, Dip?' she asked brightly, as we walked from the car to the front door.

'Yes, Felicity,' I nodded with heartfelt sincerity, 'yes, I think I probably did.'

Chapter Nine

'Why do you keep a tube of bubbles by your bed, Dip?'

My sandwich making was arrested in mid-spread by Mark's casual question. It takes a moment to focus on details of your life that have been around for so long that you never really think about them any more. They're simply there, aren't they? Besides – I felt a little embarrassed.

'Do you want me to make something up, or shall I tell you the real reason? I think I'd rather invent something.'

Glancing over my shoulder I saw that Mark's habitual expression of glowering resentment had been replaced by one of his dazzling, infrequent smiles. It was, typically, a quite startling transformation, and it revealed more than a hint of the very good-looking young man who would undoubtedly emerge eventually from the grumpy chrysalis that continually drove Kathy to such extremes of rage and impatience.

'Go on, then,' he said, slumping down on one of my creaky kitchen chairs, 'tell us the real reason.'

It was Friday, a couple of weeks after the school sports, and Mark had dropped in to visit me on his way home from school, just as he'd done a few times in the past, and rather more frequently since my announcement that I wasn't yet ready to move in with the family. Very early on I had learned that effusive greetings and bright chit-chat about his school-day were exactly what he didn't want on these occasions. Indeed, we were positively in competition over which of us could be the more laid-back and breezily nonchalant during the half hour or so that he stayed. The truth, though, as I soon came to realize, was that there was always a specific reason for these after-school visits, but the unwritten rules were quite clear. I was never to ask why he'd come, and he was allowed to choose his own moment to communicate whatever was on his mind. Once or twice he'd been unable to open up at all, and had left with an expression of baffled frustration on his dark features, furious with himself for not saying what he'd come to say. I feared for the peace of the Robinson household when that happened.

This time there was one thing I had known for sure as soon as he walked into the kitchen. He was hungry. Kathy had told me, and I had seen for myself, that Mark preferred what his mother called 'grazing', to eating. This graphic term perfectly described his habit of strolling around the kitchen picking bits off the edge of cakes, scooping stuff from containers in the fridge with his finger, tearing ragged wodges from the loaf in the bread-bin, and drinking straight out of milk and lemonade bottles without bothering to use a glass. All in all, this grazing was yet another of the annoying habits that was likely to produce almost instant aggro when he was at home. I was amused to observe, on this particular Friday, that Mark was cruising slowly around my kitchen, extending his hand in the direction of the food cupboard, then the fridge, then a chocolate cake with white icing on top that I'd left out, then the fruit bowl, and in each case suddenly withdrawing it at the last moment, as though the demands of politeness were just – but only just – managing to overcome the power of his appetite. It would have taken a harder heart than mine to ignore such plaintive, blatant need. I was bonelessly casual.

'You wouldn't fancy something to eat, would you, Mark?'

'Err, yeah – thanks.' How on earth could I have known? Desire emboldened him. 'Can I have a bit of that cake?'

'Of course, I'll cut you a slice. Will that be enough, though?'

Mark licked his lips. 'Any chance of a Sizzler?'

'Well, there might be if I knew what it was.'

I cut a large piece of cake as he explained.

'It's a special sort of sandwich thing I make sometimes when Dad's out. Mum dun't really mind me making 'em, but Dad throws a wobbly when there's a mess, and I always leave a mess. Let's make two, Dip, then you can have one.'

Irresistible enthusiasm. I put his cake on a plate and handed it to him.

'Tell you what, Mark – if I happen to have got whatever sizzlers are made of, and it doesn't take more than about ten minutes to make them, and you tell me how to do it, I'll make us one each. How about that?'

'Great! First of all you need a slice of bread.'

I patted the bread-bin. 'Got that.'

'Then you need some Marmite.'

I stroked my chin. 'Mmm, I might have to delve a bit deeper for that.' Opening the larder, I burrowed among jams and pastes and tins of this and that on the bottom shelf until, at last, my efforts were rewarded with a sighting of the familiar yellow lid. I held the marmite jar aloft in triumph. 'Got it!' I examined the jar more closely. 'Not much left, I'm afraid.'

'It's all right, you don't need much. Now we need an onion.'

'A whole onion?'

'No, you know – slices of one. You slice it up.'

'Right, no problem. Here's one in the vegetable rack. Looks a bit black and vile on the outside but it'll all peel off. Anything else?'

'Cheese.' The word elbowed its way out through a mouthful of chocolate cake.

'Cheese, did you say?'

'Yeah.'

'Any special kind of cheese?'

'Just ordinary.'

'Cheddar, you mean?'

'Yellow – ordinary. I think it is Cheddar, yeah.'

I opened the fridge and took out a block of cheese. 'There we are.' I unwrapped it and put it on the table with the onion and the Marmite. 'Let's get the bread out ready as well. How many slices are we going to need for both of us?'

'Just two.'

'Is that everything now?'

'Yeah.'

I studied the ingredients of our forthcoming snack. 'So, we've got Marmite, onion and cheese. Mark, are you sure you're not doing some undercover work for Rennie's?'

He didn't even notice my feeble joke. 'What you do now is – you toast the bread on one side, right?'

'Right.'

'Then you spread the Marmite – but not too much – on the other side, right?'

'Yes, got it.'

'And then you cut slices of onion off the – well, off the onion, only they've gotta be thin, right?'

I nodded.

'And you put the onion on top of the Marmite, and then you do the last thing, and that's putting slices of cheese on top so you can't see any of the stuff underneath – '

'Thick slices of cheese?'

'Not too thick or it goes bubbly on top too fast – and then you put it under the grill and wait till the cheese all melts together in one lot and then you take it out and eat it.' He smacked his lips and sucked air and saliva through his teeth. 'Can't wait!'

'It does sound pretty good', I agreed. 'Okay, then, you sit down and read the paper or something, and I'll see if I can produce a pair of perfect sizzlers.'

As I began to peel and slice my bruised onion I wondered how often Mark felt relaxed enough to communicate with such enthusiasm and proprietorial confidence. It may have been just the making of a humble toasted sandwich that had inspired him, but it was good to see so much animation.

'Can I look round your house, Dip? I can't get into reading the *Times*. I only really like the *Express* and *Mail* and all those.'

I didn't stop what I was doing, but this innocent enquiry sent my imagination sprinting around the various rooms of my house checking bedroom and bathroom floors for underwear or general mess or anything else that might offer embarrassing revelations about my personal life. My imagination returned, puffing and panting, to report that all was clear. I had a very stern word with my imagination later about its failure to notice the bubble mixture.

'Yes, you carry on and have a look round, Mark. After all, I've seen all round yours. I don't think you'll find it very interesting, though.'

I had just reached the Marmite-spreading phase when Mark returned with his casually expressed question. Ludicrously, I felt as if I'd been caught out in some dreadful fetish or perversion, and it was quite true that I had been on the verge of pretending that the bubbles were for Felicity, or were left over from a children's party or something like that.

'Okay, well, the real reason I keep that tube of bubble mixture by my bed is that it helps me when I start to feel tense.'

Something in the quality of the silence behind me suggested that I had struck an unexpected chord. I started to lay slices of onion neatly on to the Marmite as I continued.

'Every now and then I get – I don't know how to describe it really – I get sort of panicky and my chest goes tight and I feel as if I'm in one of those horrible little tiny prison cells where they used to cram people in the old days. Does it matter if the cheese goes over the edge, or not?'

'No, you don't want to do that or it melts all down on the grill. You mean the ones where you couldn't stand up or stretch out or anything?'

'That's right. So, when I start feeling like that I reach for the bubbles, and that really helps me.'

'How does it help you?'

My two carefully constructed sizzlers were ready for toasting now. I placed them carefully under the grill and turned the heat up to just above halfway.

'There! Two or three minutes, do you reckon?'

'Till the cheese melts sort of neatly over everything else. I usually put it on too high.'

'Okay – I think I'll sit down for a moment.' I sat next to him at the table. 'The thing is, Mark, it's just not possible to blow bubbles in a hurry. There's no such thing as urgent bubble-making. You have to blow very gently and really concentrate if you want decent bubbles. And it's just the same if you do it by waving the wand thing through the air. You have to make smooth, graceful movements with your arm' – I mimed the action – 'so that the bubbles come out in a nice regular stream.' I shrugged, feeling rather pink and silly all of a sudden. 'I s'pose it's just that after a few minutes of playing with my bubbles I – well, I settle down a little bit. Does that make sense to you, or are you beginning to think you're dealing with an absolute loony?'

'Yeah.' Mark nodded gravely, then suddenly grinned as he realized the implication of his agreement.

'I mean – yeah, it does make sense, not you're a loony. D'you like going to church, Dip?'

I haven't learned many things in my life, but one thing I have begun to understand is that when B follows A it is quite often disguised as W or even Z. In Mark's case this was particularly true. You simply had to accept that there was a sort of sub-conversational logic going on inside him, and that apparent *non sequiturs* were quite often directly linked to what had just been said. I knew that if I simply answered the question and expressed no surprise at what sounded like a complete change of subject, all would be revealed in the end.

At the same time I was very aware that this was perilous ground. I knew for a fact that Mike and Kathy were feeling very tender and guilty about what they saw as their failure to bring Jack and Mark up as enthusiastic followers of Jesus. Felicity believed everything she was told without question at the moment, but there was little evidence that either of the boys felt any real interest in the Christian faith – not, at any rate, as it was expressed and practised in our own church community.

'I have to be honest, Dip,' Kathy had said to me only a week or two previously, 'despite the fact that I've always said I'd like them to be their own people making their own decisions and all that, when it comes to the crunch I panic, and none of that seems to matter. All I want is for them to be nice, uncomplicated, incurious, card-carrying members of a chorus-singing, sausage-sizzling, sex-avoiding, Bible-studying, evangelical church youth group. I can't bear the thought that it might be me who's put them off the whole thing. Jack was converted about five times when he was little, and he used to be quite involved, but he doesn't come with us at all any more, and I'm afraid to ask him what he thinks about God in case he announces that he's an atheist. I can't bear the thought of him smiling that annoying little young-old smile of his and pitying me for my middle-aged naïvety. As for Mark – well, as you know, taking Mark to church is rather like taking a small but intense raincloud to some sunshine holiday resort. He sends out great waves of gloom and misery and boredom, and I get horribly embarrassed because of the impression he must give to other people, and then I get furious with myself for caring what other people think, and then I get wild with him afterwards for spoiling my enjoyment of the service, and he says, "Well, why do you make me come, then?", and I can't think of an answer, and Sunday goes gurgling down the plughole yet again. It's getting me down, Dip, but I'm not giving in. I *refuse* to give in – he's coming with us whether he likes it or not, and that's that!'

It was the recollection of these comments of Kathy's that caused me to pause rather lengthily before attempting to answer Mark's question. Being an honorary family member is all very well, but it doesn't give you the right to undermine decisions that are being stuck to like grim death – even if you don't altogether agree with them.

'Well,' I replied warily at last, 'it depends what – '

'I mean, what about last Sunday?' An expression of mingled anger and resentment darkened Mark's face as he spoke. 'Well bad, that was!'

I thought back to the previous Sunday. Yes, I was forced to admit to myself, much as I loved many things about my church, it had indeed been *well* bad on a number of levels, but, for me personally, that particular day had been a lot more complicated than that. Last Sunday had been . . . .

'The worse thing was,' said Mark, interrupting my musings, 'a kid in my class called Bradley Jenkins was there 'cause it was his cousin. He's been taking the . . . . He's been laughing at me about it all week. I reckon the sizzlers are done.'

They were done, and they smelled absolutely wonderful.

'Get a couple of plates out of the carousel under the corner, Mark, and a knife and fork for me out of the drawer – I don't suppose you're too bothered about cutlery, are you?'

'Tastes better with your hands', said Mark.

The sizzlers tasted as good as they smelled, and for a few moments we chewed in companionable silence.

'Tell me what you really thought about last Sunday, Dip.'

'All right, Mark, I will. I'll tell you what I really thought about it.'

It had been one of those Sunday when a christening had to be inserted into the middle of the family service. I was sitting somewhere around the middle of the church, and the Robinsons were on the back row because, consistent as ever, they had arrived late.

The inclusion of a christening in the service had its normal quota of predictable effects, the most inevitable being the transformation of Stanley Vetchley, our resident reluctant Anglican, into an even darker little cloud than Mark, if that was possible.

Two years earlier Stanley, a widower of past retirement age, had felt called to leave the small nonconformist chapel at the other end of town, a place where he and his beloved wife, Ethel, had worshipped for decades, and to become an attender at St George's instead. It was a brave piece of obedience because Stanley clearly found most Church of England practices quite abominable. Generally speaking he was able to control his negative responses to the liturgy and the communion ('Coming to the Lord's table' Stanley called it) and the 'fancy dress' worn by our vicar – indeed, we were often able to laugh with him about his reaction to these things, but when it came to infant baptism the laughter had to stop. Stanley just *knew* that was wrong, but unfortunately he didn't stay away. He turned up to signal his disapproval on each occasion in exactly the same way. Sitting bolt upright at the back of the church in his smart, double-breasted, obsolete Sunday suit, arms folded and jaw set grimly, he would refuse to communicate in anything but a graceless grunt from the beginning of the service to the end. It was like having an extra pillar in the church, one that, in its own way, was even more obstructive to some people than the ones that were made of stone.

Another common feature of christening services was the sudden increase in the number of human bodies present, particularly, for some reason, when members of the family in question were not usually church attenders. It had been like that last Sunday. More than twenty people filed self-consciously into St George's to witness the baptism of baby Samantha, and they all dressed up more smartly than most of the people who came regularly.

Particularly self-conscious on this occasion were a couple of young men in their very early twenties who had the unmistakable aura of those who have been encased into their best suits and behaviour by determined wives, mothers or sisters. They sat on the pew just in front of me, bent forward with their heads together, rather as they might have sat on one of the features at Disneyland, waiting for the ride to start in that submissively non-connected way that people do. Flicking an occasional nervous glance sideways at their unfamiliar surroundings, they comforted each other with whispered funny comments, hiding their laughter behind their hands as though they believed that jokes might be as unacceptable in church as cigarettes. Above their heads, in a phantom thought bubble, I seemed to read the words: 'If we can just sit this one out – the booze will come.'

There's quite a lot of talk in our church from time to time about the great opportunities that are presented by baptism services. People who would never normally come into a church have a chance to be exposed to the Gospel – that's the theory. In fact, we don't actually adapt what we're doing very much to suit these occasional visitors. Maybe we shouldn't change anything. Maybe we should just be what we are. I'm not sure. Sitting behind these two fellows really made me think, though.

The vicar wasn't conducting the early part of the service on this particular day. Instead, it was led by a man called Roy Taphouse who lived with his wife and two grown-up children in the same road as the Robinsons, but much farther down the hill towards the recreation ground. Roy looked rather like the film actor, Christopher Lee, but there was nothing of the vampire in him. Always kind and considerate, he was one of those people who put an awful lot of hard work into following and obeying God. Much as I liked and respected Roy, though, I found the fact that he invariably led services in a light, bright, totally optimistic, ever-cheerful sort of way a little irksome – not that I would ever have said that to him or anyone else. Lots of people loved the service to be conducted in that way, and why, I dutifully asked myself, shouldn't they have what suited them?

On this occasion Roy started with a prayer from the green service books – much flurry, page-turning and puzzlement from the uninitiated christening-attached ones – and continued with an announcement that we were going to learn a new and exciting chorus from the yellow song-books.

'I'm pretty sure we haven't tried this chorus in the past,' he enthused, 'but I heard the music group playing it through before the service, and' – he beamed roguishly – 'I have a feeling we shall be singing this one all through the week.'

Nervously, the members of the music group launched themselves severally into the beginning of the exciting new chorus, and, having regrouped a little further along the tune, led us haltingly through three attempts at one of those strangely insubstantial, fiercely celebratory songs that cause congregations to bare their teeth in determined joy. The exhausted silence that followed reminded me of a hush that descended at one of my birthday parties once, when a lot of very noisy things had cascaded from the top of a kitchen cupboard and we were all waiting to hear if one more was going to fall after a moment's pause.

It was in the middle of this silence that I overheard one of the fellows in front of me make a dispassionate comment to his friend.

'Oh, yeah, I'll be singin' that all through the week, won't I? Can't wait to get in to work down the garage tomorrow – teach all my mates that one, eh? They'll love that, won't they? We'll *all* sing it all week. That's a great song. . . . '

Prayer time followed shortly after that, conducted by Amy Bennison, an impossibly vague middle-aged lady who smiled constantly through thick, round-framed glasses and would do absolutely anything for anybody. Amy and her husband Derek, a similarly good natured, jockey-like little man, had never had children of their own, but they adored everyone else's offspring unequivocally and indiscriminately. Amy was always volunteering to help with children's groups, but had to be deflected most of the time because her enthusiasm was just not matched by her ability to maintain control. Not that the chaos she engendered caused her any personal alarm or discomfort. As far as Amy was concerned, children were simply wonderful – whatever they did. I suppose the vicar had reckoned that prayer-time was a pretty safe bet, as no little ones would be involved. He was wrong.

'I think it would be so nice,' said Amy sweetly, 'if some of the little children could come up and help me with the prayers this morning.'

A breeze of dismay ruffled the still heads of the congregation. I'm sure many of us prayed that the children would stay in their seats. But children are contrary little persons, aren't they? On those occasions when you really want them to go up to the front they suddenly turn shy or even tearful, and cling, poultice-like, to their coaxing, slightly embarrassed, vaguely annoyed parents. Not this time. This time our silent prayers of entreaty were not answered. Several small children clambered excitedly from whichever laps had been accommodating them and toddled up to cluster around dear Amy, who patted their heads delightedly, and smiled broadly at Roy Taphouse, as if to say, 'Aren't they sweet – isn't it wonderful!' Roy, who had retreated to a chair at the side, smiled back nervously. Even his eternal optimism wasn't proof against the potential disaster of any situation that involved Amy and small children.

'Now,' said Amy, addressing the congregation, 'I thought it would be so nice if our little friends here could suggest some topics for prayer, because I'm sure the things they think of will be just as important as anything that we grown-ups talk to God about. So, come along, children, what shall we pray about in our service today?'

There was silence for a moment. Most of the congregation watched and waited in a considerable state of tension. I felt like a close relative of some amateur juggler who has found himself performing at the Palladium.

Annabelle Short was the first child to make a suggestion. She spoke in a thin, squeaky voice, but with crystal-clear enunciation.

'Could we pray about the wind?'

Amy's fond smile froze for just a second as she accommodated this novel proposal for prayer. A sharp intake of breath from the row behind me suggested that Renee Short, Annabelle's elegant mother, was desperately willing Amy not to embark on a plea for the healing of flatulence in the church worldwide.

Amy's accommodation process was complete.

'Of course we can, Annabelle. Do you want to say a little prayer for us about the wind, dear?'

An even sharper intake of breath from behind.

'No', said Annabelle simply.

'Fine, then I'll say one. Let's all close our eyes and talk to God about the wind.'

Amy closed her eyes, her smile moving inwards and upwards as she addressed the creator of the universe.

'Dear God, we come before you now to pray about the wind. We thank you for the wonderful way in which it err . . . blows, and we remember all those mechanical things that go round to produce – is it water or electricity? I think it's one of those. Without the wind that you send, dear God, those things wouldn't go round and people wouldn't be able to have the water – actually I think it *is* electricity – err, they wouldn't be able to have the electricity that is produced when they do go round, so we do thank you on their behalf for the wind that you send, in all its many, err . . . facets. Amen.'

We regulars murmured a relieved 'Amen', but the two young men in front of me were bent over double, their faces buried in their hands, producing little explosive noises as they tried to control their laughter. Next to them, on the same pew, an aggressively well-behaved and hatted female, presumably a connection of theirs, glared and nudged threateningly.

'Is the wind something you're specially interested in, Annabelle?', asked Amy, her voice full of kindly interest.

'No,' said Annabelle comfortably, 'it's not.'

'I *see*', said Amy brightly, as if she'd said it was. 'Now, who else has got something for us to pray about?'

'I have.' The chunky infant voice came from a little boy whose name I didn't know, on the other side of Amy.

'What would you like us to talk to Jesus about?'

'Drizzle', said the little boy.

'Drizzle?', said Amy.

'Yes.'

'Oh, drizzle, yes – well, that's the same as rain, isn't it, dear?'

''Snot.'

'It's not?'

The infant opened his mouth wide and, in a husky monotone, delivered one of those mechanically abrupt, computer-like emissions of newly acquired knowledge that small children specialize in.

'Rain-is-when-you'd-get-really-wet-if-you-went-out-to-play-and-drizzle-is-when-you-might-be-able-to-go-out-and-play-soon-'cause-it-prob'ly-won't-last-long-so-just-be-patient.'

'Well, I think we'll pray about rain for now, dear, because I think they really are the same, you know.' Amy shut her eyes. 'Dear God, we thank you for the rain that – '

The infant burst into tears. 'Don't wanna talk to Jesus 'bout r-r-r-rain! Wanna talk to Jesus 'bout d-d-d-drizzle!'

'All right, dear,' said Amy hastily, 'we'll say a prayer about drizzle. No more crying now.'

The infant's crying shuddered to a gasping halt. He passed the back of a small hand across his tear-streaked face and gazed expectantly up into Amy's face.

'Dear God,' prayed Amy, still smiling, but with just a hint of desperation in her voice, 'we thank you for the drizzle that falls down on us from the sky. . . . '

The pattern was set. There was no going back now. Those children were determined that every meteorological condition they had ever encountered or heard about should be presented before the throne of the Most High. We thanked God for the snow, the hail, the thunder and the sunshine. We also thanked him that none of us had been killed in earthquakes or drowned in floods. The whole episode was like something out of a comic novel, especially as it became increasingly clear that Amy didn't know how to stop. As the children gained confidence their eyes gleamed with the knowledge that an adult was dancing to their tune. They grew much more competitive and deluged her with weather-related subjects for prayer. Fortunately, just after we had prayed that the little clouds wouldn't get hurt when they bumped into each other, Roy had the sense to intervene at last, and the children returned to their parents' laps in a state of extreme excitability. Amy went back to her place beside Derek, still beaming, clearly convinced that it had all gone very well indeed. I noticed that Derek smilingly nodded approval and laid a hand over his wife's as she sat down. I felt a little pang of jealousy. Amy had someone who would always tell her she'd done well. What did it matter if she was a bit vague and deluded? I felt depressed suddenly.

'I wish they'd pray for a job for me.'

It was one of the young men in front who had addressed these words to his companion. He spoke quite quietly, and had obviously not meant anyone to overhear what he said, but I was taken aback by the passion in his voice. My depression increased as I asked myself what this man must think of the service he had been corralled into attending today, a service in which nothing that had happened so far had any identifiable relevance to the life he led or the people he knew or the things that were important to him. I wished, as I had wished so many times in the past, that Jesus could be here in the flesh, sitting among us, answering questions, healing those of us who were sick, telling us off when we were silly or wrong or presumptuous, praying for a job for this young man . . .

I wish they'd pray for a job for me.

I couldn't get those words out of my head as the service went on, led now by the vicar. All through the christening section, while the parents and godparents mumbled miserably that, yes, they *did indeed* turn to Christ, they *did* repent of their sins, they *did* renounce evil and they *did* believe and trust in, not just one, but all three persons of the trinity, that one sentence returned to me again and again. By the time the final blessing was being said I had descended into an all too familiar morass of self-pity and judgementalism. Why should I go on coming to this useless church where no one seemed to understand how to relate to a real world full of real needs? Why did we let Stanley Vetchley get away with sitting there in a big sulk just because he didn't happen to like what was happening? Why did the vicar allow people like Roy Taphouse and Amy Bennison, sweet-natured though they were, to be a public expression of what we claimed to believe? What was the use of it all? Why couldn't Jesus be here with us to sort it all out?

It was while that final blessing was being said that a few words from the New Testament slipped in through the merest fissure in my self-absorption. I certainly wouldn't have let them come in and spoil my sulk if I could have prevented it. They consisted of a few words from the end of Matthew's gospel, and a verse from that wonderful section at the end of John where Jesus is talking so passionately to the disciples before his arrest.

Behold I am with you always. . . .

But I tell you the truth, it is for your good that I am going away. Unless I go away, The Counsellor will not come to you, but if I go, I will send him to you.

When I opened my eyes the vicar was inviting everybody to stay to coffee in the hall attached to the church, and the two chaps who had been sitting in front of me were standing up with a purposeful, 'Let's get out of here' look about them.

I came so close to chickening out. Everything in me wanted to go and get a coffee and a biscuit and chat comfortably to someone who would make no demands on me, but I had said that I wanted Jesus to be here to pray for a genuine, practical need, and he was – in me.

Come on, Reynolds, put up or shut up.

I found them just outside the church. The rest of their party were still inside, presumably drinking coffee and eating biscuits and showing off baby Samantha, but these two were standing happily in the sunshine with newly-lit cigarettes, deeply inhaling the smoke, like drowning men who have found an air supply just in time. I cannot tell you how difficult I found it to begin my conversation with them.

'Err, excuse me, you don't know me,' I began breathlessly, 'but I was sitting behind you in church just now during the service, and there was something I just wanted to say to you . . . err, if that's all right?'

'What, did we leave something behind?' said the slightly more affluent-looking one who had mentioned the garage he worked in.

'Oh, no no, nothing like that, it was just that . . . well, I couldn't help overhearing something.' I looked into the eyes of the tall, skinny, large-featured young man with the spiky haircut who was responsible for my present embarrassment. 'It was something *you* said.'

'D'I say something wrong?' he asked, glancing over his shoulder with a trace of alarm at the church doorway through which those who policed his life might pass at any moment.

'Good heavens, no! Of course not. No, it was after the children had said all those silly prayers about weather, remember?'

'Oh, yeah.' He looked down, grinning, avoiding his friend's eye and stirred the gravel with the toe of his boot.

'It's all right, I thought it was very funny as well – for a while, anyway.'

He glanced up into my face, focusing with sudden wariness on the strangeness of my approach to him. 'What'd I say then?'

I took a deep breath. 'You said something like "I wish they'd pray for a job for me". In fact, I think that's exactly what you said – "I wish they'd pray for a job for me". You did say that, didn't you?'

His face turned a dull brick-red colour. 'Might've said something like that. What about it?'

'Well, I wanted to offer to pray with you now – if you'd like me to, that is. We could ask God to find you a job.'

He waved an arm towards the church. 'I'm only here for Sammy's whatsit. I don't belong – '

'You don't have to belong to the church. We can just talk to God here and ask him.'

He looked helplessly at his friend, desperate for guidance in this highly specialized area of acceptable ways in which to respond to strange females who invite you to pray with them outside churches. The friend rolled his eyes, shook his head, and shrugged with equal helplessness.

'Might as well have a go', he said doubtfully. 'You might get one.' Then to me, 'Put our fags out, shall we?'

A little bubble of hysteria rose in me and popped into a chuckle.

'No, it doesn't matter about your cigarettes. God won't mind that. We'll just talk to him now. What's your name?' I asked the brick-red one.

'Err, Michael Edward Simmonds – Mick.'

'Mick, right. Let's pray, then.'

Awkwardly, the two men bowed their heads and clasped their hands in front of them like footballers preparing to block a free kick in front of goal. Smoke curled up in two grey columns from the cigarettes held between their fingers, adding an oddly ceremonial atmosphere to the triangular proceedings.

'Father,' I began, straining to believe in miracles, but woefully conscious that my faith seemed to be draining out through my feet, 'we want to ask you about a job for Mick. We know there aren't many jobs around nowadays, but if there's something that would really suit him – '

'Dun't matter what it is', qualified Mick gruffly, and rather surprisingly. He was obviously anxious for

God to be quite clear, that, far from being fussy, he was in the market for anything that was going.

'If there is something he could do, Father – anything at all – he'd be really grateful, and so would I, and so would his friend here.'

'Steve', mumbled the friend informatively into his tie.

'So would Steve. Thank you for what you're going to do. Amen.'

After that we shook hands solemnly, and I went back into the church, leaving Mick and Steve highly relieved and lighting up fresh cigarettes to replace the ones whose smoke had carried our prayers up to heaven. As soon as I was back inside I became aware that my legs had turned to jelly, and I had to sit down for a while to recover. I had done it, though! Feeble, faithless, fearful and judgemental I certainly was, but I was so glad that I had done it!

'Well embarrassing!' exclaimed Mark, who had listened to my account of last Sunday's service with rapt attention. 'Glad I wasn't them.'

'Glad you wasn't who?'

'The two blokes – Mick and the other one. Praying out in the street where everyone can see – *well* embarrassing! D'you think he'll get one?'

'A job, you mean?'

'Yeah.'

'I think God can do anything he wants. I just hope he wants to give Mick a job. I can't bear the thought of running into the poor fellow in the High Street over and over again if nothing happens. *Well* embarrassing for both of us, wouldn't you say? Anyway, that's what I thought about church last Sunday. It was pretty terrible, but I was part of the terribleness, so I can't really criticize.'

'You know you said you have the bubbles because of getting tense?'

'Mmm.'

I sensed that we had arrived at the reason for Mark's visit.

'I get tense.' Mark's eyes dropped. He began to draw on the tablecloth with his finger.

'What about?'

'Lots of things. Mum getting cross and saying I don't listen, and her not listening when I try to say things. And she says I ought to be nice but I can't when it happens – the words don't come out. I have to wait till I can do it differently.'

I leaned back in my chair – people like Mark are drawn, not pushed. 'Do you mean that you feel all the things she thinks you ought to say, but you can only show it in ways that are more doing than speaking? I haven't put that very well, but is that more or less what you mean?'

Mark nodded and a huge tear plopped on to the plate that had managed to catch a few of the crumbs from his sizzler. He jammed the heels of both hands into his eyes and rubbed hard until they were reddened and tearless.

'I want Mum to let me stop going to church, Dip. It's boring an' embarrassing an' it goes on for ever. Jack's allowed to stay at home. None of my friends have to go, an' they all think I'm stupid for going. It ruins all the week for me thinking about it coming an' messing up the weekend, an' then it comes an' it's awful. I know Mum wants me to look as if I'm liking it, but I can't. I hate church. I hate Sunday! I really *hate* it!' He paused. It wasn't difficult to guess what was coming next. 'Will you talk to Mum an' ask her if I can stop going? She won't get cross with you.'

'Hmm. . . . ' I found myself puffing my cheeks out and drumming with my fingertips on the tabletop – a clear sign that I was out of my depth. 'Mark, I can't simply ask her to let you stop going – not just like that. I'm sure that wouldn't be right. Anyway, it's not just your mum. Your dad's got to agree as well, hasn't he?' I did a bit more puffing and drumming and shot silent, panic-stricken prayers into the ether as I tried to decide what to do for the best. 'What I can do, if you want me to, is talk to your mum and dad about what you've said, and tell them you're really, genuinely upset about going, and not just making a fuss, and then I'm afraid I'd have to leave it to them to decide what do do.'

Mark stretched his arms up straight above his head, linked his fingers and yawned as if he was in the last stages of exhaustion. Then he dropped his arms into a folded position on the table, shivered abruptly from head to foot, and sniffed loudly.

'Could you talk to them soon, Dip, please?'

'I'll pop round and have a chat tonight if you like. Are you all right, Mark? Is there anything I can get you?'

That smile again. 'Wouldn't mind another bit of chocolate cake.'

Chapter Ten

I spent a couple of hours at the Robinson's later that evening. We talked in the kitchen while Jack was watching television in the lounge. Mark was out with his mates and Felicity was staying the night with her friend Claire Elphick.

I described to Kathy and Mike how Mark had dropped in, I talked about the success of our culinary adventure, and I went on to convey – or to try to convey – the passion with which he had expressed his negative attitude to church services in general and last week's in particular. I was careful to mention Mark's single tear, hoping that even that tiny amount of liquid would be enough to dampen the fire of what was likely to be an automatically angry reaction from Kathy. In conclusion, I made it clear that I was not taking an advocate's role, but simply passing on a message, as it were. When I'd finished they were both still and silent for a while. Finally, Mike leaned back sighing deeply and ran both hands through his thinning hair.

'Thank you, Dip,' he said quietly, 'you're a good friend.' He looked worriedly at Kathy whose gaze, wide-eyed and trance-like, was fixed on a little red wooden top of Felicity's that she was twirling endlessly between thumb and forefinger. 'I don't think there's any doubt that we have to respond to this, Kath, wouldn't you say?'

'Have to respond', echoed Kathy dully, her eyes still fixed on the object in her hand. 'What a very splendid idea – yes, we shall certainly have to respond to this, shan't we? We shall devise a suitable response, and then we shall – well, we shall respond with it, and everything will be all right. All quite simple, really.'

'I didn't say it would be simple.' Mike's voice had become even more hushed, but it was not the hush of peace. His tone was muted by apprehension and growing annoyance. 'I just meant that we can't pretend we don't have a problem. We have to do something about it, and whatever we do has to be thought through properly. I really hope that, just for once, we can take a short cut and avoid all the emotional stuff so that we come up with something that's right for Mark and within God's will. I don't see how the logic of that can be faulted.'

Kathy thrust her left hand up in the air and, with her right, spun the top into whizzing life on the table. It shot across the pine surface, bounced against the edge of an uncleared supper plate and twizzled drunkenly back towards her. She caught it and set it spinning again.

'Please, sir,' she said, speaking in a little girl voice and flapping her raised hand as if to attract attention, 'please, sir, can I have permission to tell you how the logic of that can be faulted?'

The muscles in Mike's jaw tightened. He laid an arm across the base of his chest, rested his right elbow on his left wrist and scrubbed wearily at his face with his free hand. Meanwhile, the red top, having bypassed the plate this time, flew across the table and fell to the floor at Mike's feet. Kathy pushed her chair back with her bottom and ducked under the table-top to retrieve it. Mike clenched his teeth and burst in a contained sort of way.

'Could you *please* stop playing with that stupid thing when we're supposed to be discussing something as serious as – as our children's church attendance! *Please!*'

Delighted with such signal success in making Mike play schoolmaster to her naughty child, Kathy scrambled back into her chair in simulated panic, and placed the recaptured top down beside her with exaggerated, finger-tip care before sitting up nice and straight with her arms folded. An infant 'being good'.

'Sorry, sir – won't do it again, sir. Don't hit me, sir!' Didn't mean it, sir. Permission to tell you now why I can't take a short cut and avoid the emotional stuff, sir?'

Nobody said anything for a moment. Boringly, I had yet another of my 'should I be somewhere else?' hot flushes, but I couldn't bring myself to say anything. No lines had been written for a third character in this particular sketch. But Kathy, whose perceptions, like most agonizers, can sometimes be very dulled but occasionally are very keen indeed, must have registered some twitch or change of colour or involuntary sound on my part. She dropped out of role for a moment, but she didn't look at me.

'Please don't go away, Dip. Part of me – not a very nice part, I'm afraid – wants to kill you for being someone Mark says things to because he thinks he can't say them to me without me boiling over and not really listening. But another part of me is glad he did.' She paused and swallowed. 'I honestly am. I'm glad. I just wish – I just wish I'd done it all better. . . . '

Kathy's eyes looked so sad and lost that both Mike and I extended a hand towards her involuntarily. She took Mike's.

She took Mike's – one flesh.

'We don't have to go through any more of this, Kath,' said Mike gently, 'I'm sorry – say whatever you want to say.' He smiled ruefully. 'We'll do it my way next time we get married.'

'I'm always saying you should have married that Miss Rendell from your school office,' said Kathy, blinking away some unshed tears, 'she'd have recorded details of her wedding night in triplicate and sent a copy to all close relatives – very efficient and unemotional. Item number five – consummation satisfactorily completed at eleven forty-nine precisely.'

'Kath!'

'I'm sorry too, Mike. We waste an awful lot of time playing our rubbishy little games, don't we? But I can't just coolly discuss things like this as though they don't affect me – you know I can't.' She shook her head slowly as if in disbelief at what she found within herself. 'The pain is so awful – so *bad*. It cuts into me and makes me feel I'm going to fall over or something, not physically, but in some other unspeakable way, some fundamentally collapsing, nightmare-come-true sort of way. And there's nothing I can do about it, there's nothing to rub on it, nothing powerful enough to distract me from it. Even Boots haven't got anything to make it better – except sometimes in the music section, I suppose, and that medicine's expensive nowadays.' She looked at the ceiling, fighting back fresh tears, and spoke very slowly and clearly. 'It really does hurt very much indeed, Mike. I know you find it extremely irksome when I give in to these feelings – '

Mike made a noise that seemed compounded of apology, impatience, slight embarrassment and sympathy. 'Kath, it's not that I don't – '

'And I don't blame you,' continued Kathy, adding for the sake of absolute veracity, 'well, I know I *do* blame you, but I shouldn't – I really shouldn't. Because it's not your problem, Mike. It's nobody's problem.' She swung a hand towards me. 'It's not Dip's problem, it's not Jack's problem, it's not Felicity's problem, and it's certainly not Mark's problem. It's mine. It belongs to me, and I ought to keep it in a sock under the bed.' She smiled a watery smile. 'Can you keep psychological pain in socks under beds, do you think, Dip?'

'No space left under my bed', I replied. 'Care to have a look sometime?'

Care enough to have a look?

Kathy smiled again. 'All right, fair exchange. We'll swop problems. In fact, why not go a step further? Why shouldn't we be the very first people to introduce the concept of neighbourhood Neurosis Parties – make a change from tupper-ware, wouldn't it? We could all sit around oohing and aahing over each other's obsessions and manias, and pass the latest "Knit Your Own Delusion" kit round while we're sipping our coffee and nibbling our thin slices of Valium Gateau. The sky's the limit after that. How about a mail order catalogue called *ANGST*, offering easy terms on the very latest straitjackets in pretty pastel shades of powder-blue, leaf-green and salmon-pink? We could make a fortune. We could – '

She broke off as Jack, humming idly, came into the kitchen with an empty glass in his hand. He studied our three faces calmly as he took a bottle of milk from the fridge and filled his glass, then he took a gulp, swallowed it down and nodded knowingly.

'Heaveeee, right?'

'Enjoy your milk, Solomon.' There was no offence in Kathy's tone.

Jack must have read something in his mother's face, or perhaps he just saw the tears in her eyes. He leaned down and planted a milky kiss in the middle of her forehead.

'Take it easy, Mumsy,' he drawled, in a broad American accent, 'I'll be next door ready to come in with both guns blazin' if these here varmints start any trouble.'

He winked at Mike and me as he went out, closing the door quietly behind him.

'I'd say it was you varmints who need the protection', said Kathy, dabbing her eyes and her forehead with the tea-towel that Mike passed her. 'What is a varmint? I've often wondered.'

'I think it's wonderful that Jack feels free enough to give you a kiss like that in front of other people, Kathy. A lot of parents would give their eye-teeth to have that kind of relationship with a son of his age. You must have done a few things right.'

Mike murmured agreement with me, but I sensed that they had been over this ground many times before.

'Oh, I'm pathetic, Dip.' Kathy threw the tea-towel in the direction of the rack and missed. Mike got up and hung it neatly back where it belonged. 'Suddenly I feel all right again because one of my children did something warm and nice. It's ridiculous to keep swinging from one mood to another – absolutely ridiculous. As you're standing up, Mike, can we have a glass of sherry now that I don't need one?'

Mike busied himself with glasses and crisps and nuts and bowls. I wanted to know more about how my friend became so tender in the first place.

'Kathy, what exactly is the pain you were talking about? Why does Mark and church and him not being able to say things to you make it quite as bad as it was just now?'

There was a long pause before she answered. Mike put the drinks and nibbles before us, then sat back down in his chair without saying anything. Kathy sipped her drink and gazed across the top of her glass into the distance.

'I got injured, Dip. A long time ago, when I was little, I got injured. Believe it or not, I can hardly remember how. I just know that life was a blur of uncertainty and tension and things going wrong whenever you got excited about them going right. I used to have the same dream – well, nightmare really – over and over again when I was a small child. I would be at a party or a film-show or a picnic or something really nice, but I would know that just as I was beginning to really enjoy myself the *voice* would whisper in my ear.'

'The voice?'

'A sad, disgusted sort of voice – not disgusted with me, I don't mean, but with life, with everything. I hated it.'

'What did it say?'

'It always said the same thing – the same words every single time in this horrible hoarse whisper. "Black curtain time", that's what it said, and in the dream my heart would sink like a stone and I'd be filled with terror and try to move towards the other people but my legs wouldn't move, and then a thick, black, velvety curtain would fall with a flapping, swishing, cynical thud between me and all the light and noise and life, and I'd try to get through it but I never could, and I'd scream in the dark and wake up sweating and gasping for air as if I was suffocating.' She peered at her hand, curled round the stem of the sherry glass. 'You know – I haven't told you this, Mike – but I realized the other day that every time I think about that part of my life my teeth clench and my hands curl into fists, and all the feelings and memories come back as though it was yesterday instead of years and years ago.'

'What sort of memories?'

'Well, I suppose the ones that come back most are

all those evenings I spent sitting on the landing wrapped in my bedspread listening to Mum and Dad arguing and shouting downstairs. I used to follow every word they said, straining with all my might to *make* the power of my wanting affect what they were doing to each other. That's the trouble with being little, you see. You believe what grown-ups say, so when you hear your mother screaming that she's going to walk out and never come back, you don't understand that it's just another move in a sort of wild game of emotional chess. You believe it. Every single time – you believe it. I came down from my room once, after she'd said that, because I'd heard the front door open and slam, then it all went very quiet and I thought she really had gone. I could hardly breathe with the fear and panic inside me as I went down the stairs. I was going to tell my father that he had to go after her and get her back and promise her there wouldn't be any more rows.'

Mike asked quietly, 'What happened when you got downstairs, Kath?' I felt a moment of surprise that he had never heard this story before.

'Well, nothing really, that's what was so awful. Mum was doing something to the washing machine in the kitchen, and Dad was in the sitting-room watching *What's My Line?* on television. I still have this mental snapshot in my memory of grumpy old Gilbert Harding in a brown box spouting off about something or other. I was so taken aback by my mother being there and not having gone after all that I didn't know what to say. This little engine of fear inside me was suddenly roaring away without actually engaging with anything. It was a most odd feeling, and part of it was a totally uncomprehending childish anger towards my mother for creating such panic in me and then not doing what she said she was going to do, even though I didn't want her to do it. *Well* rational, eh?'

'So what happened in the end?'

'Oh, this is a real multi-Kleenex-job, Dip. I ended up getting told off for being rude, would you believe? When Mum spotted me palely loitering out in the hall she said, "What are you doing down here at this time of night?", and there was just no way I could turn all those feelings into words, so I let the anger in me talk. And *it* said, "I'll come downstairs whenever I want and you can't stop me". Of course, the roof fell on my head after that. Mum told Dad what I'd said, and they suddenly found – surprise, surprise – that they did have something in common after all. They were both very cross with me, and I was shot back to bed and told I was a very naughty little girl. I lay and raged in the dark for ages – but I was glad my mum hadn't gone.

'I understand a lot better now, of course. My parents had their problems just as we've got ours, even if most of them are completely different ones. But the things you learn when you're a kid are facts, even if they're not facts. And the constant, gut-twisting uncertainty of those times, the feeling that everything's bound to end in disappointment or conflict or disaster of one kind or another – that's what the kid in me still knows for sure is the way the world really goes. That's the injury I was talking about and it's never had a chance to heal properly. Any sort of failure with the children just opens it up again and it hurts as if it had only just happened.'

Kathy drank the last drop of her sherry and placed the empty glass suggestively beside the bottle on the table. Mike did pour more sherry for us all, but, rather to my private annoyance, only a very little into each glass. One day I shall murder someone who takes it upon him- or herself to monitor my alcohol intake.

'When I became a Christian,' continued Kathy, 'I thought somehow that everything would work out okay in the end. Because God was on my side my marriage would be successful, and the kids would grow up believing the same as we do – whatever that is – and the past wouldn't be allowed to keep reaching out and grabbing me by the throat and spoiling everything. I wasn't quite sure how all that would happen – I just assumed that it would. I really was quite naïvely optimistic about the future, but I think now that I got it wrong. God hasn't got rid of the problems – he hasn't scrubbed out the inside of my life with a divine abrasive cloth and left it shiny and germ-free. Right deep down I think I'm glad he hasn't. I want to be me, and I want him to be *in it* with this ragged, turbulent me. I just wish – ' She sighed wistfully. 'I just wish he could have stretched a point and made the kids want to go to church with us. Just now, when you passed on what Mark had said, Dip, it was Black Curtain Time again and I couldn't handle it. Silly really, isn't it? So!' She bounced the palms of her hands on the table. 'There we are. That's why we can't take a short cut and avoid the emotional stuff, Mike. There's too much of it to find a way round. I have to burrow right through the middle. And if you ever pour me a third of a glass of sherry again I shall go on to meths, and so will Dip, won't you, Dip?'

'Yes,' I said solemnly, 'I probably will. Kathy, I was just thinking – thanks, Mike – I was just thinking, bearing in mind all that you've just said, that you must find it difficult sometimes to work out whether you're an amazing success as a mother, or a miserable failure.'

She blinked. 'What do you mean?'

'Well, you've got this bag full of weights that you drag around with you everywhere you go, and it's invisible, so no one really knows how much effort is involved in just keeping going. But you have kept going, and considering the size of that handicap – '

'You make me sound like something not worth backing in the three-thirty at Haydock Park.' Kathy is hopeless at handling any kind of compliment.

I pressed on doggedly. 'Considering the size of that handicap you've done an amazing job, and I think you should be proud of yourself.'

And so should I, shouldn't I?

'It is an interesting thought,' responded Kathy, driven by embarrassment into whimsy as usual, 'that the time will come when God will press the Show All Characters button on that great computer in the sky and every one of us will be revealed for exactly what we are. There'll be me staggering around with my ton of garbage wrapped up in a big black curtain,

and there'll be Mike tripping along with a small neat
attaché case, containing small neat problems inserted tidily into appropriate compartments.'

'If you think being married to you is a small neat
problem that can be inserted tidily into an appropriate compartment you can jolly well think again!'

Mike's indignant explosion was so comical that we
both burst into laughter. He looked a little offended
for a moment, then laid his head on his shoulder and
smiled sheepishly, like a small boy.

'What you say about Kath is quite true, Dip,' he
said, 'she does do a great job with the kids – I've
been trying to tell her that for years. I know I get
annoyed and fed-up sometimes, but that's because I
honestly do find it very difficult to identify with all
this burdens-from-the-past stuff. I know it's all quite
real,' he added hastily, raising both hands as if to
ward off attack, 'but, you see, I had a genuinely
happy, well-organized childhood with Christian parents – my mother can be a bit fierce, as you know,
but very kind and loving – and I guess I'm always
trying to make it like that here. I get just as upset
about the boys' attitude to church as Kath does, but
I'd rather take the problem straight to Jesus, and
then make some practical decisions. I guess we're
just made very differently.'

Vive la différence!

'What are we going to do, Mike?'

'You say a prayer, Kath.'

'Me?'

'Yes, you. Put all your care for them into a prayer.'

Kathy showed her teeth and widened her eyes in

pretend horror. 'Now? Out loud? I think you or Dip would be much better at praying about this than me. You're both calmer – more rational, you had happy childhoods. . . . '

Did we?

'Oh, all right, Mike. You don't have to look at me under your brows like that any longer. I'll pray.'

In the silence that fell just before Kathy began her prayer I experienced one of those strange moments of almost complete peace. The other two had closed their eyes and bent their heads, but I kept my eyes open as I usually did nowadays, and gradually became conscious that something unusual was happening. Familiar objects and surfaces in the kitchen had acquired something that I can only de-scribe as a luminosity – a greater, shining reality, and the warmth of – what can I call it? – of sheer Presence, was rippling gently through the air and through my own body, producing the kind of un-earthly intoxication that seems to inflame the spirit rather than the mind. So rare, those times, and so valuable.

'Father, it's me, Katherine – Kathy, I mean. We want to talk to you about our children, Jack and Mark and Felicity. You know how much' – Kathy's voice broke a little, ' – you know how much we adore them, and how much we want to do the right things for them, and you know how we – I – keep on failing because I get so upset and those horrible jagged feelings get in the way of what I know I ought to do and say. Please – oh, please don't let it be held against them if they move away from you because of me. Forgive me for the times when I give in to the feelings inside me, and help me to be stronger and – and more obedient. You know what it's like to have a son, and watch him going through difficult, terrible times and not be able to do much about it, don't you? Oh, Father, doesn't it hurt to be a mum or a dad. . . . ' Mike retrieved the tea-towel and put it into Kathy's hands again. She mopped and sniffed and recovered. 'We've got to decide what to do about church now, Father, and we don't really know what to do for the best, so we just want to ask you to be with us and help us and guide us, because we're a bit lost at the moment – well, I am anyway. Look after them, love them, be real to all of them one day. Thank you very much – goodbye.'

For some reason, Kathy's involuntary and slightly confused substitution of 'goodbye' for the more traditional 'amen' brought the tears to *my* eyes. It was so plaintive somehow. For what must have been a full minute after that we sat and savoured the atmosphere that had been created by Kathy's prayer. Then Mike spoke at last.

'You all right, Kath?'

She took a deep breath and blew it out again loudly. 'Fine – thanks for the tea-towel, Mike. I'm beginning to feel rather fond of this square of cloth. If we ever come across a home for broken-down tea-cloths this faithful old friend shall spend the autumn of its life there, instead of being torn into strips and used for unmentionable things. What do we do now?'

'Well, I'm no more certain about anything than

you, but I suggest we get Jack and Mark together before Sunday – '

'Not Felicity?'

'No, I wouldn't have thought so, would you?'

'No.'

'Would you have thought so, Dip?'

'No.'

'And we'll ask them quite quietly and openly what they think about it all. We'll make it quite clear that they can say whatever they like.'

Kathy nodded sombrely, then leaned forward and glanced around the kitchen as if to check for eavesdroppers. 'All right,' she whispered, 'but we won't mean it, will we?'

Chapter Eleven

The planned meeting took place on the next day, Saturday. I met the Robinsons by arrangement at their house when they returned from a whole-family walk up on the 'bosomy hills' as Kathy termed the gentle chalk range that lay a few miles to the south of our town. I knew that Mark was always keen to get up into the hills, mainly because he loved to fly his kite, one of those big, manoeuvrable ones with two control lines attached to plastic handles. He had let me have a go now and then in the past, and I must admit it had bubbles beaten into a cocked hat – it's a bit tricky flying a kite in your bedroom, though. . . .

The sky had been piled high with heavily laden clouds all day, and rain was just beginning to spatter against the windows when the clang of van doors shutting, thumps, clatters, flapping noises, one high-pitched voice and mutual recriminations on a slightly lower register announced the family's arrival at their front door.

The 'plan', carefully worked out by Mike, Kathy and me, was that I would have a really nice tea prepared and laid out in the sitting room, and that in this convivial, post-ramble, familial setting it would be much easier for the boys to speak openly and freely about church-related matters. The problem of Felicity had been solved, in theory, by hiring a video of *Three Men and a Little Lady*, her favourite film of all time ('all time' being six years, of course) which she was to watch on Jack's portable set upstairs, with her own special tea laid out on a tray. Felicity received the news of this arrangement with hand-clapping delight, switching abruptly to deep suspicion.

'What are you all going to be doing in the sitting room when I'm upstairs, then?' she asked, after I'd described what was happening.

'We're going to be saying things we don't want you to hear,' I replied, 'but not about you.'

The frankness of this explanation made her giggle, and she was soon settled in front of the television, a corned-beef sandwich in one hand, a glass of orange squash with one of those twisting, coiling plastic straws in the other, her eyes fixed adoringly on the screen as those three wonderful men appeared.

Meanwhile, in the sitting room, the warm, familial setting was obviously turning out to be rather less convivial than Mike and Kathy had hoped. I arrived at the bottom of the stairs to find Mark at the front door explaining grumpily to two of his friends that he wasn't able to come out because his parents were making him stay in to have tea when he didn't even want any tea, but that he'd come out as soon as he was allowed to, so why didn't they wait just outside the front door until then. At this juncture Kathy appeared at the sitting-room door, furious but icily polite.

'There's no point in asking your friends to wait,' she announced, 'because we don't know how long we shall be, do we?'

'Don't wait.'

The friends drifted off into the rain, and Mark

stomped back to the sitting room. I closed the front door and followed him.

'Well, this is nice', said Mike a few minutes later, though it palpably wasn't. Everyone was drinking tea and eating, including Mark, who had miraculously regained his appetite, but the general atmosphere was strained, to say the least.

Jack was sitting on the floor with his back against a glass-fronted bookcase containing one or two books and several stuffed-in, unclassifiable piles of papers and magazines. He finished a mouthful of sausage-roll, brushed a few flakes of puff-pastry from his pullover onto the carpet, and addressed his father.

'Come on then, Dad, let's have it.'

'It?'

Jack gestured widely with one arm. 'All this. Dip's done this great tea, Flitty's been packed off upstairs, Mark's not been allowed to improve the situation by going out – '

'Nobody thinks you're funny, Jack.'

' – and you and Mum are sitting on the edge of your chairs trying to look casual and relaxed and as if you haven't got something special to say when you obviously have, and Dip's trying to look as if she doesn't know what it is – and now she can't help laughing because she knows I'm right, so you might as well get on with it.'

Mike and I were both laughing as Jack reached out a languid arm to secure another sausage roll, but Kathy wasn't. Nor was Mark. The two of them would have made very poor company for Napoleon on those long Elba evenings. Mike laid his plate gently down on the occasional table beside him.

'You're quite right, Jack,' he said, 'we do want to talk to you both about something, or rather we're hoping that you might say a little bit to us. It's about church and what we – you believe about God and Jesus and all those things. Those things have always been important to us, as you know, but we'd like to know what you think. Jack doesn't come to church with us at the moment and we don't try to make him – well, we wouldn't want to at your age, Jack. But we've never really spoken about it, have we? It's one of the faults Mum and I have got – just letting things drift more than we should, I mean. And Mark still comes, and obviously doesn't really like it, and that's not much good, is it? So – ' Mike drummed a rhythm on his knees with the flat of his hands in a slightly nervous fashion ' – we just wanted to clear the air a bit, that's all. You can say whatever you want – anything. And we won't, you know, get upset or anything.' He glanced at Kathy for confirmation. 'We won't, will we, Kath?'

'No,' said Kathy, shaking her head over-vigorously and looking very upset, 'no, we won't.'

Mark, who had quite deliberately perched himself on a hard, uncomfortable wooden-backed chair near the door, threw an urgent question at me with his eyes, but I just smiled back as noncommittally as I could, and hoped that he wouldn't ruin his own chances of getting what he wanted by making some typically ill-considered comment at this early stage of the proceedings.

'So,' continued Mike, 'who's going to be first?'

Something told me that Jack was extremely unlikely to open up in front of his brother. In fact, during the seemingly eternal silence that followed Mike's speech I seriously doubted that either of the boys was going to say anything at all. A glance around the room did not reassure me. Mark had stopped eating and was leaning forward with his elbows on his knees, his face scrunched between his fists, Jack was well into his second sausage roll, apparently quite relaxed, but with little lines of thought wrinkling the space between his eyebrows, and Kathy had flopped back into the corner of the sofa, one bent arm resting high on the back of the seat, her hand covering her eyes. Only Mike looked comparatively serene, now that his first little attack of nerves had passed. Sitting on the other end of the sofa from Kathy with his legs neatly crossed, his eyes moved expectantly but calmly from Jack to Mark and back again, like a teacher who is quietly confident of his ability to control. Surprisingly, it was Mark who broke the silence in the end.

'I don't mind God but church is crap.'

This ungracious but obviously sincere comment had a near-disastrous effect on me, particularly as I had a mouthful of vanilla slice at the time. I don't know why I found it quite so funny, except that as soon as Mark had spoken I formed a mental picture of Almighty God seated majestically upon his throne, receiving that harassed angel whose task it is to monitor the progress of the Robinsons. 'What news of the boy Mark?' the creator of the universe would enquire impressively, and, as the mighty hosts of heaven leaned forward in solemn expectation, the angel would reply, 'He says he doesn't mind God but he thinks church is crap'. Perhaps my view of God's nature is a mistaken one, but I suspect that, far from dipping automatically into the thunderbolt box, he might have smiled a little to himself on hearing this, and said, 'Well, first of all, it is, of course, immensely flattering to hear that Mark doesn't mind me, and, as for the second point, well, I wouldn't have put it quite like that myself, but the lad has a point – he certainly has a point.'

Fortunately, I managed to prevent the involuntary distribution of my vanilla slice and to keep a straight face, which was just as well, because neither Kathy nor Mike had found anything amusing about Mark's comment. Kathy whipped her hand away from her eyes as soon as the word 'crap' issued from her youngest son's mouth, but, presumably not trusting herself to speak, simply turned to Mike with a 'Get The Thunderbolts Out' expression on her face.

'I hear what you say, Mark,' said Mike, adding the restrained rebuke, 'but I don't think you needed to use that word to say it.'

Don't you just hate it when people tell you they hear what you say? For one fleeting moment I really wanted to hit Mike, but then, I'm not a parent.

'It's not as bad as what Mum's said to me sometimes, an' anyway, you said we could say anything we wanted', protested Mark. Then, after a moment of fierce concentration, 'All right, then, church is boring and goes on for ever and I hate it. I mean, I hope that bloke gets a job an' that, but that was outside church, and inside's *well* grim.'

I made a mental note to explain Mark's obscure

reference to 'that bloke' to Mike and Kathy afterwards.

'If I was God I wouldn't go', continued Mark. 'Mum, *please* let me stop going.' His tone had switched suddenly from aggression to supplication, and I sensed that this was far from being a mere strategic move. He was actually offering, as a kind of hostage, the vulnerable part of himself that he knew his mother yearned to have access to. 'I can't stand it any longer. I feel all big and red and ugly when I'm sittin' there. Don't make me go any more – I'll do the dinner washing-up every Sunday instead.'

This implicit equating of church attendance with household chores brought a smile to Mike's face, but all of Kathy's spirit was gone. She seemed to have sagged into complete defeat. When she spoke to Mark it was with the weak submission of one who sights inevitable surrender. She barely had the energy to speak.

'You're quite right, Mark,' she said faintly, 'I have used some awful words when I've been angry with you, and I'm really sorry about that – I always said I'd never do that with my children. Please forgive me for doing that, and for shaking you and smacking you sometimes when I run out of words. . . . '

Mark moved uncomfortably on his chair and mumbled something that, although quite unintelligible, carried with it faint nuances of both apology and forgiveness.

'I hope you know, Mark,' went on Kathy in the same energy-less tone, 'that God is very important to me. I think Jesus died for me so that God could be my Father, and I've been trying to understand what that means ever since I – well, since I became part of it. I mess things up all the time in all sorts of ways, but right deep down inside I think I know I love God, and he loves me – although I lose my way a bit with that sometimes. So, what I'm saying is that, however it might seem, even if the church blew up tomorrow morning and I couldn't go any more, there'd still be God and Jesus and me. It isn't just how it looks to other people – although I'm afraid that seems to really matter to me sometimes – it's about me hoping you'll know God as well one day. That's the only thing that matters in the end.' She looked at Mike. 'I think we ought to let Mark stop coming to church for the moment, except for Christmas and things – only if you agree, of course, Mike.'

The cessation of breathing from the chair by the door was louder than the breathing had been.

Mike nodded judicially. I stuck an invisible plaster on the place where I had wanted to hit him earlier. 'I'm happy to go along with that,' he said, 'as long as Mark is quite clear that this is a decision made by us, and that we shall expect there to be no argument on those occasions when we do require him to attend church with us.'

Despite being addressed by his father as if he was an applicant at some land tribunal, there was no doubt that Mark understood what was being said. It was lovely to watch. He sat bolt upright in his chair and stared open-mouthed at his mother, hardly able to take in the fact that his weekly torture was over.

'So I don't have to go tomorrow?'

'You don't have to go tomorrow', she confirmed, in the same weak voice that she had used before.

Mark, driven to an excessive show of emotion by sheer relief and excitement, crossed the room at a most un-Marklike speed and threw his arms round his mother's neck. 'Oh, thanks, Mum!' Those were, I think, the words that emerged in a rather muffled state from this unexpected embrace. The miraculous effect on Kathy, though predictable to anyone who knew her, still amazed me. It was as if she had been instantaneously and totally healed, like one of those New Testament sufferers who encountered Jesus. One sudden, substantial dose of physical and verbal affection, when she had thought the medicine bottle might be empty, and her whole being was transformed. As Mark disengaged himself I saw that her eyes were shining and her body had ceased to sag. When she spoke her voice had regained its strength and vibrancy.

'You can probably catch your friends up if you hurry', she said, pretending to push him away. 'It's no use expecting Jack to say anything while there's any food left, so you might as well go and spread the joyous news.'

'All right.' Mark, grabbing the shining moment, headed for the door, pausing only to say, 'Thanks, Mum – thanks, Dad.' Just before disappearing he flashed one of his film-star smiles at me – a real sizzler it was. After that we heard hurried coat-flapping noises as he got ready to go out in the rain, and then there was a short silence during which I believe (and I would bet quite a lot of money on this) that, in the solitude of the hall, Mark raised his eyes, bent his arm, and shook a triumphant fist towards the ceiling, this being the gesture that traditionally accompanies the universal victory cry of the fourteen-year-old.

'Yes-s-s!' we heard him cry exultantly. 'Yes-s-s!'

Then the front door opened and didn't close again, and he was gone.

'I'm glad you let Mark go.' Jack was speaking to his mother as I came back in after shutting the rain out. 'I couldn't have said what I really thought if he was here. I'm afraid I can't stand him at the moment – he makes me feel about thirteen, and I start saying childish, stupid things that I'd never say to anyone else.'

Kathy shook her head and sighed wistfully, failing to register, perhaps, that Jack's analysis of his relationship with Mark almost exactly described her own. 'Such a shame. The two of you used to be such good friends. He called you Jackypot when he was a very little boy – '

'Thanks for remembering that, Mum. Cheers!'

' – and he thought you were the most wonderful person in the whole world. You and he spent hours together in the garden making up stories and building dens down behind the shed.' She smiled as a particular memory surfaced. 'And I'll never forget once in the summer, when we were on holiday in Dorset, down in that very quiet place beginning with "K" that was difficult to get to because we hadn't got a car then, remember? One day we went down to one of the beaches you could get to by walking through a cornfield from our cottage. A lovely twisty walk. There was no sand or anything like that when you got down to the seafront, but there were loads of rock-pools. You loved it, Jack. You always loved rock-pools.'

'Still do', murmured Jack.

'There you were as usual, picking your way between the rocks, turning over stones in the water, and every now and then you'd look up and shout that you'd found a crab, or a little fish or a prawn or something, and we'd be really impressed, wouldn't we, Mike?'

Mike smiled and nodded. Jack took the last vanilla slice and bit into it with a resigned air.

'And just behind you,' Kathy was totally immersed in the past now, 'little Mark was toddling along as best he could, turning over much smaller stones because he wasn't as strong as you, and peering into the water as hard as his little eyes could manage, desperately wanting to find something that he could call out about just like you'd been doing, and he wasn't having any luck at all.'

'That's right,' interrupted Mike, leaning back and signalling sudden recall with a wagging finger, 'and he got so fed up with not coming across anything real that he decided to inject a little creativity into his research, so – '

'He turned over yet another rock,' interposed Kathy, who hates to be deprived of a punch-line, 'and he looked up to where we were sitting at the base of the cliff, and he shouted, "Mum! Dad! I've found somefink!" And I shouted back, "Oh, good, darling – what is the somefink you've found?" And he shouted back, "It's a camel! I've found a camel! Look, Jackypot, I've found a camel!"'

Jack chewed and nodded, remembering. He swallowed and said, 'Well, I suppose from Mark's point of view it seemed just as reasonable that he might find a camel as any of the other things I'd been shouting about. After all, he couldn't have known what most of them were anyway.'

'And you started clambering over the rocks towards him,' continued Kathy, 'then all of a sudden I saw that wonderful proud smile fade away from Marky's face, because he'd realized that when you got to his pool there wasn't going to be any camel to see, and he said in this small, troubled voice, "Well, I tort I saw a camel". I got all frantic, remember, Mike? I flapped my arms about trying to attract your attention, Jack, and I couldn't because you were too busy making sure you didn't slip on the rocks. But the lovely thing was that it was all right anyway because when you reached him you looked down into the pool and then you shouted up to us, "Heh, Marky's right! There *is* a camel in his pool, but it's gone under a rock now, so you won't be able to see it." Oh, Dip, you should've seen that little boy's face when he knew his big brother was backing him up. So happy and pleased! That was so typical of Jack, Dip – such a kind little boy. I remember, just before we moved down from London, we had two cats, and Jack was really worried that – '

'Mum!' Jack rolled his shoulders against the bookcase in embarrassment. 'We're not going through every event in my entire childhood, are we? I don't like that kid I used to be. If I'm honest, he makes me shudder. I've been trying to get rid of him for some time now. I don't need reminding about the little twit, and especially not about all his clear-eyed, piping heroics. Can't we throttle him once and for all?'

People are funny, aren't they? Mark only had to twitch an eyebrow for Kathy to react strongly in one direction or another, but this speech of Jack's, devastating as it sounded, just made her laugh. By contrast, Mike, who could handle anything that Mark threw at him without becoming unduly troubled, looked deeply distressed and puzzled by what he had just heard.

'I don't follow you, Jack,' he said, leaning forward and frowning, 'why on earth should you mind about having been that sort of child? I really don't understand.'

Jack had the look of one who having started down some perilously steep cliff-side, wishes he hadn't but discovers that there is no possibility of going back. He screwed his face up, trying to find words to express what he was feeling.

'Don't get me wrong. It's not that you haven't been good parents', he said.

Oh, dear. . . .

'It's just that I think you wanted me to be a sort of – I dunno, a sort of Enid Blyton boy, an honourable, manly little chap who isn't afraid to look the world in the face, and, apart from a few rather endearing little naughtinesses, always does the right thing, whatever that is. You taught me to think that being like that was the best way for a person to be.'

'Something of a caricature, Jack?' suggested Mike very quietly. 'And I'm afraid I still don't understand how the qualities you just mentioned could be regarded as some sort of handicap – rather the opposite, I should have thought.'

'But that's just it! That's just the word. A handicap, that's *exactly* what it was.' Jack accompanied this uncharacteristically vehement speech with a series of rhythmic punches, one fist upon another. 'What you don't understand, you see, is that Enid Blyton boys have a very tough time when they find themselves in the middle of real life, especially if real life turns out to be the kind of secondary school I went to. You get crushed and bashed and laughed at, and at first you can't work out why it's happening to you. Your mum and dad, who are the people you trust most, have told you that if you're good and kind you'll be happy. It turns out to be not true. If you stand up for what you believe in people are going to respect you. Not true. If you try hard with your schoolwork you'll feel happy about yourself. It's not true. Everything will be all right in the end, because everything can be fixed by Mummy or Daddy or God, but it can't. It isn't true. It may be true if you're not an Enid Blyton boy. If you were a sort of King David boy who's faced a lion or two you might manage to cope with the odd giant, because you'd know from early on that things *do* get difficult, and you'd be a bit more ready for them. Well, I wasn't ready, and I didn't cope.'

Mike's face looked grey. 'I know you had some difficult times at school, Jack, particularly in the fourth and fifth years, but most children – '

'Dad, you're not hearing me. I'm not saying I had a terrible childhood. I didn't. We had lots of fun and good times, and I know you and Mum love me, and I love you both very much.'

'So what's the – '

'It's just that – ' Jack spread both hands wide and closed his eyes ' – it's just that I think, in a funny sort of way, you used me as a little museum – a place where you could keep your ideals, and your moral values and your religion all shined up and carefully placed and untainted by the mess and untidiness that surrounds them in your lives – in *real* life, I mean. But the trouble is, they're yours, not mine, and I have to throw some of them out and smash a few others and keep one or two, and get some you never thought of, and make a bit of a mess of my own, and generally – well, make it all real for me.'

Vibrations of feeling double-bassed through the air.

'Yes, the trouble is, Jack,' replied Mike, his voice very carefully controlled but heavily laced with pain, 'that when you talk about wanting to – what is it? – throttle the child you used to be, you're talking about one of the most wonderful, magical periods of my life.' Mike's words fell on our ears with the softness of cotton wool being dabbed on a grazed knee. 'It really does hurt me that you want to dismiss it – just chuck it away, as though it's worth nothing. It *can't* have been worth nothing, can it?' He shifted his weight on the sofa. 'You know, I used to think that the way you are, all the good qualities in you – and they are there, Jack, even if we got lots of it wrong – I used to think it was, well, it sounds so silly when I say it out loud, I used to think it was the best thing I'd ever done.' He stared into the distance for a moment. 'I wish I hadn't said that now, it does sound very foolish indeed. I'm sorry.'

'No, I'm sorry,' said Jack, looking rather pale, 'I

wasn't going to say all that – ' He checked himself '– not because it isn't true, but because it's only one part of the truth. And I overdid it a bit trying to be clever. I promise you I wouldn't have wanted any other parents, and I'm very happy to be me. Dad –'

Drawing his feet in, he levered himself up from the floor with one hand, and moved across to his father, who was still staring into the distance as if stunned by the discovery that some fundamental law of the universe was not immutable after all. Jack leaned down and put his arms around Mike, who jumped slightly, but responded straight away, patting his son's back with one hand as if he was trying to bring up wind.

I think that silent cuddle poured a measure of reassurance into Mike. As he watched his son return to his seat on the floor, he blinked a little and wiped his glasses on a soft green cloth that he produced like a conjuror from his top jacket pocket. Kathy shoved along the sofa and linked her arm in her husband's. Kathy has two main modes, whatever she's really feeling, one is tragedy and the other is flippancy.

'Well, we are having a torrid time, aren't we?' she said to no one in particular. Then looking at me, 'What do you think of the story so far, Dip? "Stress Family Robinson". Better than *East-Enders* or *Coronation Street* any day, wouldn't you say?'

I shook my head. 'I'm just so impressed with you all. I mean – Kathy, you worry about not having the perfect Christian family, but you're way ahead of the one I grew up in. I know you argue and get cross with each other and go through all sorts of problems, but you really love each other as well, and every now and then you even *say* so! The nearest my father ever got to telling me he loved me was those rare occasions when he didn't actually tell me to clear off.'

Don't let them home in on that – this is not the time.

I laughed lightly. 'But don't get too sad, that was pretty much par for the course in the part of the world where I grew up – and my dad was one of the more demonstrative ones. The nearest some of my friends got to being told they were loved was not being belted.'

Okay.

'I was supposed to be telling you what I thought about Christianity and all that', said Jack. 'Do you still want me to?'

Kathy groaned wearily and laid her head on Mike's shoulder. 'Oh, Jack, I don't know if I can handle any more true-life revelations at the moment. You're not going to tell us you're a closet satanist, are you? I couldn't stand it.'

'No, Mother,' replied Jack patiently, 'I am not a closet satanist. In fact – if anything, I suppose I'm more of a closet Christian than anything else. Do you want to hear about it?'

Mike's eyebrows had shot up at Jack's use of the phrase 'closet Christian'. He nodded briskly, very interested. 'Yes, of course we do. Tell us what you mean, Jack. We'd really like to know where you stand nowadays.' (Mike did plunge from time to time, but he was always happiest hopping from one little island of cliché to another.)

'Well, I won't go on and on about it,' said Jack, 'but what I was going to say before all this childhood stuff came up was that I guess I stopped going to church every week for three reasons, one that really meant something, or I thought it meant something, anyway, and two very bad ones. I won't bother to tell you the bad ones – '

'Oh, yes you will, Jack Robinson,' interrupted Kathy with some asperity, 'you don't get to make us feel inadequate and deeply impressed at the same time with your deep philosophical arguments until we've heard the miserable, shameful little confessions that are probably the real reason you stopped going. Come on – give!'

Jack giggled embarrassedly, and I thought how much he looked like Felicity. 'Oh, all right, Mum. If you must know, the first one was that – '

'You didn't like getting up on Sunday mornings?' suggested Mike shrewdly.

'The first one was, as you so rightly say, that I didn't like getting up on Sunday mornings,' agreed Jack, 'and the second was to do with the quality of the coffee they used to serve – and presumably still do – through that little hatch in the hall after church. Do they still do that?'

'Yes, they do', said Kathy. 'Do I take it that we're coming on to the reason that really meant something now? Something deep and significant to do with the coffee?'

'No, Mother, we are coming on to the second of the very silly reasons, as you well know. Because I always found it so difficult getting out of bed on a Sunday morning, I was almost invariably up just in time to get to church only if I ran *very* fast. This meant that I missed out on the first cup of coffee of the morning, the one that turns me into a human being. So I'd sit through the service, trying to banish all these lurid fantasies about steaming hot mugs of strong, sweet coffee, and failing miserably, and then when the service was over we all went through to the hall to actually *have* a coffee, didn't we?'

'We did.'

'And every single time I tried to convince myself that for once they would use decent coffee granules, and that said cup would be just a tiny bit more than half-filled with water that might have actually boiled at some point in its history.'

'Water boiled – coffee spoiled,' quoted Mike boringly, but he added, 'well, you're right really, the church coffee is pretty awful.'

'Yes,' said Jack, 'especially for someone like me, who's been brought up by his misguided parents to believe that the only coffee worth drinking looks like something dredged out of the Black Lagoon, has half a field of sugar-cane dissolved in it, and comes in a container the size of a chamber pot.'

'Hear, hear!' I said, with deep feeling.

'Thank you, Dip. As I was saying, for a long time I was a believer. Every Sunday I had faith for change.' Jack gestured with his hand towards heaven like an old-style preacher and raised his voice to evangelizing pitch. 'Friends, I knew in my *heart* that the coffee would be good, and I refused to believe the voice of the deceiver telling me that no good thing would ever come out of that hatch. Hallelujah! I *refused* to believe the evil one! However,' Jack switched abruptly to his normal voice, 'it soon became clear that on this occasion the evil one was absolutely right. The coffee was uniformly and unfailingly vile. I went through a period of dark, yearning agnosticism as I tried to make sense of my shattered faith, but in the end I just couldn't stand the hypocrisy of it all – going through to that hatch every week, mixing with all those bright-eyed others who still believed, knowing in my heart of hearts that they were deluded, that good coffee was just a pleasant illusion that gave people a reason to keep going through the hardship and drudgery of the church service. In the end I – ' Jack pretended to choke on his words ' – I had to stop going, and now,' he looked up with an expression on his face that was, I think, supposed to approximate to a brave smile, 'I have found a kind of peace.'

There was a short pause.

'You know, Jack,' said Kathy, dispassionately reflective, 'I really, really wish I hadn't insisted on you telling us about your two bad reasons for giving up church. How long is it going to take to tell us about the good reason?'

'Not long, Mum, I promise. Right, the good reason was that I had to have a break from being a Crimean Christian.' He raised a hand slightly in Kathy's direction. 'I am going to explain, Mum, just give me a chance. I've thought about this. You know how in the old days the army used to dress up for battle in just about the most unsuitable gear you could possibly imagine? Most of it was much more decorative than practical, and those poor old foot soldiers in particular must have got so hot and uncomfortable when they were supposed to run and dodge and fight and do whatever soldiers have to do. They were trapped,

really, in a load of traditional stuff that had no connection at all with what was going on, or the job that
actually had to be done. But I don't suppose it occurred
to many of them to complain about it, because that was
just the way things were, and you'd have needed to be a
real lateral thinker to picture it any differently. Well, I
began to feel a bit like that in our church. It wasn't that
I stopped believing in God or Jesus. I know you're
always joking that I was converted five times when I
was little, Mum, but one of them must have stuck,
because I've never stopped believing that I – I'm afraid
I don't find it all that easy to talk about – I've never
stopped believing that I belong to him, if you know
what I mean.'

Mike nodded, his face suddenly full of happiness.

'I just needed some time', went on Jack, 'to see what
would happen if I took the old traditional uniform off
and wore something more comfortable – more suitable,
if you like. After all, the British army did that a long
time ago – changed the gear, I mean. I'd hate to think
the Church hasn't caught up with the army! Dad, I
know this must all sound a bit self-centred, but it's not
just about me. We've got to be able to wear camouflage
sometimes, so we can fit in with the world. We've got to
be able to adapt and be flexible even though the reason
for joining up in the first place stays exactly the same.'

I wish they'd pray for a job for me . . . .

'And what have you found out about life without the
uniform, Jack?' asked Mike.

'He's there,' said Jack quietly, 'he's there whatever
you wear, wherever you go. He's always there – church
or no church – he's simply there. And I think he's

beginning to teach me that I'm here as well.' He smiled at his father. 'He's my God now, Dad, just as much as he's yours. The Enid Blyton boy and the Crimean uniform, both chucked out, so that I can be me, and that's what he wants, thank goodness. Oh, and since we started talking this evening I've got an idea there's something else he might want as well.'

Kathy and Mike looked at each other, and prepared for the best or the worst. 'Yes?' breathed Kathy.

'Well, I don't mean I've had any voices in my head or anything like that, but I just have a feeling it would be right for me to start coming to church again, at least now and then, in any uniform I want, as long as I'm there – but I still don't have to pretend that I like the coffee.'

Kathy stared. 'Are you telling me that you're coming with us tomorrow?' She sounded exactly as Mark had done when he learned that he didn't have to go.

Jack nodded brightly. 'That could be possible, Mumsy.'

I don't know if Jack's decision was motivated by conviction or kindness, but it didn't really matter. Kathy was *so* pleased. She passed a hand across her brow.

'Glory be, we've lost one and gained one back! The mathematics of it are beyond me. I feel a bit giddy, Mike. Pour me a small, full glass of sherry, will you?'

Beaming all over his face, Mike headed for the kitchen. He didn't pause in crossing the room, but as he passed the bookcase his hand rested for the merest fraction of a second on the top of his son's head.

Chapter Twelve

Let history record that Jack Michael Robinson did indeed attend church with his parents on the day following that conversation, but let it also record that on the following Sunday he did not so attend, for reasons more self-indulgent than philosophical. Kathy didn't really mind, though. Her oldest son was back in the fold – had never actually left the fold – and even his occasional appearances in the visible portion of the fold were to be a source of great pleasure to her.

Mark began to enjoy Sundays as well, although he kept a very low profile on Sunday mornings, fearing, probably quite rightly, that his mother's generous gesture could be eclipsed in an instant by fury at the sight of her youngest son settling down with toast and orange juice in front of the television just as the rest of the family were setting out for church.

I joined the Robinsons for lunch on that second Sunday, a day in which, for an hour or more in the middle of the day, the sun shone brightly through the merest crack in a leaden sky. I loved the lighting effects that resulted. Brightly coloured things like Daffodil, my mini, seemed artificially vivid against the slate-grey, and the hundred-year-old brickwork of Mike and Kathy's house glowed richly red, possessing an almost edible texture. It felt like a day when something exciting ought to happen. And, I'm pleased to say, it did. It rained.

Just after two o'clock, when Mark and Felicity were dealing with the dirty dishes – having Felicity's assistance with the washing-up was generally reckoned to be the short straw of short straws – and the rest of us were hopefully awaiting reluctantly promised coffee in the sitting room, heaven opened and rain flung itself to the earth as though it frantically needed to escape from the sky. So abruptly did the deluge begin, and so loud was the sound it made, that Mike, Kathy and I all stood up, more or less involuntarily, and moved across to the window that overlooks the back garden. Through the cascading downpour only the vaguest outlines of trees, bushes and neighbouring houses were visible.

'God's putting the house through a giant car-wash,' murmured Jack, 'isn't it wonderful!'

It was at this moment that Mark and Felicity appeared in the doorway, their faces alive with excitement and anticipation.

'Rain walk!' exclaimed Mark.

The dynamics of family life are very strange, but they can be very precise, can't they? Instead of looking at each other, Mike and Kathy looked at Jack, and I knew somehow that, though none of them would have recognized it, the decision about whether to accept Mark's suggestion or not depended entirely on how the older boy reacted to the idea. Rain walks, I guessed, were some kind of lapsed family tradition. Jack would have to 'bend' towards his temporarily estranged younger brother if the tradition was to be resurrected.

'Great!' said Jack. 'Let's get the stuff!'

As I followed the general stampede towards the kitchen, Mike explained that when the boys had been younger the whole family had discovered the delights of not only accepting rainy weather, but actively setting out to enjoy being in the middle of it.

'You watch them when they get out there,' he said happily, 'they go completely mad.'

First of all, though, the hunt was on for wellingtons, waterproof coats and umbrellas. If the Robinsons' bathroom was chaos, the cupboard under the stairs where these things were theoretically kept was chaos cubed. Anxious to get out before the rain eased off, the family attacked the jumbled mass of footwear and clothing as if their lives depended on it, sending up a veritable fountain of discarded items behind them as they burrowed. Assuming, correctly, that I would want to come along, Kathy, flushed with the hunt, produced a pair of green wellies that fitted me at a (literal) pinch, together with one of those old-fashioned thin plastic macs that button right up to the neck and come down as far as your ankles. Topped off with a fisherman's sou'wester held on by a strap under the chin, my outfit was not the stuff of fantasies, but it was just right for the weather.

Leaving the rejected things outside the cupboard where they'd landed, the washing-up half done, and two or three lights on, we piled out of the front door into the teeming rain, to the accompaniment of loud war-whoops from Mark and Jack who, within seconds of being outside, threw off such headwear as they'd found, tilted their heads back and ran along the footpath, allowing the water to soak their faces and drench their hair. Felicity watched her brothers with amazed delight, and looked a question at her mother. Failing to see anything like a negative reaction, she pushed back her red waterproof hat so that it hung by its strap around her neck, and ran as fast as her rubber-booted feet would carry her after the two boys, shouting at the top of her voice, 'I'm doing it too! Jack! Mark! I'm doing it too! Look – I'm wet too!'

'I used to try to stop them,' said Kathy, moving closer so that her umbrella augmented my sou'wester, 'but they never took any notice, so I gave up. And it never seemed to do them any harm anyway. In fact, the hot bath together when they got back was one of the bits they liked best. Nowadays, of course, it'll be an argument about who gets to use the bath first.' She sighed. 'I loved it when they were little. More fun.'

'Doesn't look much different to me,' said Mike, who was walking on the other side of me beneath a huge, highly coloured golfing umbrella, 'they're still going as loopy as they always did. And look at Felicity – talk about a drowned rat.'

The rain had lessened a little by the time we reached the bottom of the road, but it was still beating an urgent rhythm on our umbrellas as we followed the three revellers through a small metal gate into the recreation ground, and watched Jack lead a flight of different sized human aeroplanes in big wheeling circles around the grassy expanse. There was, by now, no greater wetness than their wetness, and they were ecstatic. The wheeling stopped, there was a brief confabulation between the three aircraft, then Mark ran across to us, his face washed and lightened by rain and joy.

'We're goin' over to play on the kids' things,' he announced breathlessly, 'but we've *all* got to go on 'em. Come on!'

Without waiting for a response he dashed off to catch up the other two, who were running hand-in-hand towards the enclosed children's playground at the far end of the recreation ground, a place that Felicity and I knew very well. We followed Mark at a more sedate pace.

'Jack and Mark are technically too old to go on playground equipment', said Mike stolidly, his voice sounding oddly hollow in the rain-free space under his umbrella.

Kathy shrieked with laughter. 'Oh, Mike, you'll be the death of me!' she spluttered. 'We're probably the only people in the universe who are out of doors at the moment. The police might have chosen today to launch a massive operation for the arrest of over-aged playground users – is that what you're worried about? "Ah," they'll have said, up at the local nick, "a monsoon. Just what we've been waitin' for. Should catch a fair few this afternoon – come on lads!" I expect there's loads of them there now, crouched under the slide, hiding inside the roundabout, disguised as climbing frames – they're all trained to do that, you know – and there'll be loads more just squatting in the long grass at the edge, waiting for whoever's in charge to blow a whistle so they can rush out and warn Mark and Jack that anything they say will be taken down, wrung out, and used in evidence. You crack me up sometimes, you really do.'

'It was only a comment,' said Mike mildly,

'anyway . . . . ' He stopped and looked at Kathy with a new light in his eyes. 'Are you prepared to put your money where your mouth is?'

Kathy and I came to a halt as well. 'Always', replied Kathy untruthfully.

'All right, then.' Mike slowly and deliberately lowered his umbrella, passed it to me, and let the rain fall on his bare head until it was streaming down his face. 'Last one on the roundabout's a cissy!'

He galloped off in the direction of the playground at a wellington-hampered sprint, watched by a momentarily amazed Kathy, who, half a second later, thrust her umbrella into my hand as well and set off in giggling pursuit. By the time I reached the wooden fence that surrounded the playground area the whole family had abandoned themselves to shouting, splashing, squealing, rain-soaked enjoyment of the weather, the equipment and each other. Mike, bedraggled and happy as I had never seen him, stopped halfway up one side of the climbing frame, and shouted in my direction.

'Come on, Dip – join us!'

They looked so complete.

'Where do you hide a leaf?' Father Brown once asked his friend, Flambeau. 'In a forest', was the answer. Where do you hide a tear? In a rainstorm . . . .

Too much standing outside fences holding things for other people. Far too much, for far too long. I stuck both umbrellas into the ground, threw off my absurd sou'wester, and joined them.